"Call me Noah."

"I can't do that, lieutenant," Kit replied tensely.

He shot her an amused glance. "Sure you can."

Kit jerked to a halt and faced him. "This isn't a date we're going on, lieutenant. I was assigned to interface between Narc and the Coast Guard. You're my boss."

Noah put his hands on his hips. Damn, but she was contrary! "That's right, I am your boss. And a little civility is in order."

Stung, Kit glared at him. "Look, Trayhern, you can cut the flirting act. I handled five tough years in that drug jungle they call Dade County, and I can handle you—and this assignment."

Cocking his head, Noah studied her. "You think I'm flirting with you?" he asked curiously. Her quicksilver temper intrigued him, and he liked her boldness. Of course, professional conduct must rule—but for just a moment Noah sensed the potential danger in letting himself think of Kit Anderson as a woman....

Dear Reader:

Stellar is the word that comes to mind for this month's array of writers here at Silhouette **Special Edition**.

Launching a gripping, heart-tugging new "miniseries" is dynamic Lindsay McKenna. *A Question of Honor* (#529) is the premiere novel of *LOVE AND GLORY*, celebrating our men (and women!) in uniform and introducing the Trayherns, a military family as proud and colorful as the American flag. Each *LOVE AND GLORY* novel stands alone, but in the coming months you won't want to miss a one—together they create a family experience as passionate and moving as the American Dream.

Not to be missed, either, are the five other stirring Silhouette **Special Edition** novels on the stands this month, by five more experts on matters of the heart: Barbara Faith, Lynda Trent, Debbie Macomber, Tracy Sinclair and Celeste Hamilton.

Many of you write in asking to see more books about characters you met briefly in a Silhouette **Special Edition**, and many of you request more stories by your favorite Silhouette authors. I hope you'll agree that this month—and every month—Silhouette **Special Edition** offers you the stars!

Best wishes,

Leslie J. Kazanjian,
Senior Editor

LINDSAY McKENNA
A Question of Honor

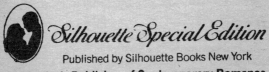

Silhouette Special Edition

Published by Silhouette Books New York

America's Publisher of Contemporary Romance

SILHOUETTE BOOKS
300 East 42nd St., New York, N.Y. 10017

ISBN: 0-373-09529-5

First Silhouette Books printing June 1989

Printed in the U.S.A.

Books by Lindsay McKenna

Silhouette Special Edition

Captive of Fate #82
*Heart of the Eagle #338
*A Measure of Love #377
*Solitaire #397
Heart of the Tiger #434
+ A Question of Honor #529

*Kincaid trilogy
+ Love and Glory series

Silhouette Intimate Moments

Love Me Before Dawn #44

Silhouette Desire

Chase the Clouds #75
Wilderness Passion #134
Too Near the Fire #165
Texas Wildcat #184
Red Tail #298

Awards:

1984 Journalism Award for fiction books from the Aviation/Space Writers
    Association for *Love Me Before Dawn*, Silhouette Intimate Moments
    #44

1985 Journalism Award for fiction books from the Aviation/Space Writers
    Association for *Red Tail*, Silhouette Desire #298

1987 *Romantic Times* Best Continuing Series Author Award for the Kincaid
    trilogy, Silhouette Special Edition (#338, #377, #397)

Waldenbooks Romance Bestseller:

1985 *Texas Wildcat*, Silhouette Desire

LINDSAY McKENNA

spent three years serving her country as a meteorologist
in the U.S. Navy, so much of her knowledge about the
military people and practices featured in her novels comes
from direct experience. In addition, she spends a great
deal of time researching each book, whether it be at the
Pentagon or at military bases, extensively interviewing
key personnel. She views the military as her second family and hopes that her novels will help dispel the "un-
feeling-machine" image that haunts it, allowing readers
glimpses of the flesh-and-blood people who comprise the
services.

Lindsay is also a pilot. She and her husband of fifteen
years, both avid "rock hounds" and hikers, live in Ohio.

LOVE AND GLORY: BOOK ONE

The Trayherns

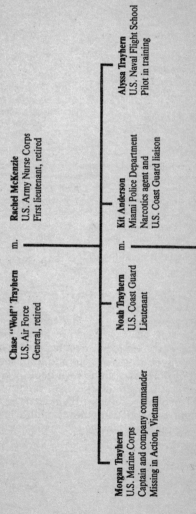

Chase "Wolf" Trayhern
U.S. Air Force
General, retired

m.

Rachel McKenzie
U.S. Army Nurse Corps
First lieutenant, retired

Morgan Trayhern
U.S. Marine Corps
Captain and company commander
Missing in Action, Vietnam

Noah Trayhern
U.S. Coast Guard
Lieutenant

m.

Kit Anderson
Miami Police Department
Narcotics agent and
U.S. Coast Guard liaison

Alyssa Trayhern
U.S. Naval Flight School
Pilot in training

Melody Sue Trayhern

Chapter One

May, 1975

There's no way you can talk me into taking this job, Chuck," Kit said tightly.

"We'll see, Detective Anderson," her superior shot back. He pushed a sheaf of recently signed papers forward to emphasize his intention. Chuck Cordeman's blue eyes caught and held Kit's gaze as she stood tensely on the other side of the desk. "You wanted to get away from the scum of Dade County, sweetheart, and you got your wish. This new assignment is yours." His gravelly voice softened slightly. "Narc division is a lousy place for anybody. And for a woman . . ." He shrugged his meaty shoulders, rounded by the weight of responsibility after fifteen years on the police force. "I sympathize with you, Kit, but this is the best I could come up with." He nudged the documents closer to the edge of the desk.

Kit reached hesitantly for them. "What's the assignment?" she asked tiredly.

Chuck's face brightened, and he sat farther back in his well-worn chair. "Congratulations, Kit. You have just officially joined the Coast Guard as an adviser. You're gonna act as liaison between their department and ours." A small grin tugged at his mouth. "You're gonna learn how they drug-bust at sea. I hope you don't get seasick easily."

Her eyes narrowed in disbelief. "The military?" she croaked as she slowly began to read the orders before her.

"You're now officially part of the South Florida Task Force," Chuck continued. "You'll interface as a member of both the Drug Enforcement Agency and the Coast Guard." He smiled slightly. "And you thought you were getting out of the excitement."

Despair caused Kit's already aching stomach to feel as if it were on fire. She ran her hand across it, trying to ease the pain. "I don't want a lateral transfer, Chuck!" Her nostrils flared. "I want out of narc completely. I thought I'd made that clear."

Chuck held up his hands in self-defense. "Listen, Kit, I tried. Honest I did. But—"

Kit's lips felt stiff with anger.

"The captain said you were too damned good to lose. Let's face it, you've been one of our best undercover agents. You've survived when others haven't. You're bright and young—not to mention that you're part of a police family. The captain sees you going places with the department.''

''Over my dead body!''

''Easy, Kit. I know how you feel. Everybody in narc gets a gutful at some point.'' His voice became soothing. ''Look, the captain likes your work. You've busted your tail and made some damned fine collars. Now you're getting this cushy assignment to take the pressure off you. Believe me, Kit, *everybody* has been bidding for this job. Hell, I'd rather chase smuggling dope boats into our country than get shot at every few days by some junkie in Dade.'' His eyes glittered. ''Wouldn't you?''

Kit clamped down on her rising anger. *Turn it inside,* she told herself. *Don't show any emotion.* Wasn't that what she'd learned from five years of living in the trenches as a narcotics agent? Show any emotion and you were on a morgue slab faster than you could snap your fingers. Her stomach burned as her ulcer acted up again. But Kit had more immediate concerns. She eyed her boss.

''Chuck, I told you—I want out. Out of narc. Out as an undercover agent. I can't take it anymore.''

Chuck shook his head. ''Everybody here develops either stomach ulcers or permanent migraines—or both. It comes with the territory. I'm tellin' you, Kit, one more year in narc and Cap will promote you to that desk job you've been wanting. Just hang in there.''

Kit sighed. Maybe he was right. Her father would be disappointed if she quit an assignment. Hadn't she and her three brothers all followed his footsteps into police work? Family tradition came first, her Irish father had gravely told her the day she'd been accepted to the Florida Police Academy.

Focusing her attention back on Chuck, Kit couldn't muster any anger toward him. He was a rumpled, solidly built man with a weathered face. That face had seen a lot of action, she reflected. Beneath that lined flesh were hidden scars born of ten years in the narc trenches. Somehow he still belonged there, even though he'd been allowed to move up the ladder to the safety of a desk job.

She cared for this man. He would never say, "Kit, I know you're hurting. I know you're tired. And I'm worried about all the weight you're losing." Chuck only knew how to be supportive by being gruff. But she knew he cared for her. Kit sighed.

"It's a one-year assignment, Chuck? Are you sure?"

"Yeah, just one. You were chosen because you're the only one who can identify Garcia, the Colombian kingpin, on sight. Word's out that he's going to be making a big drop either here, the Bahamas or Puerto Rico. We want him, Kit. Real bad. And so do you. All you have to do is cruise around on this cutter and check out every druggie they bust." He managed a sliver of a smile. "You'll get one hell of a nice tan. Most of their work is done during daylight. Hell, you'll be able to live like a normal human being, sleeping nights and working days instead of the other way around."

A corner of her mouth quirked. "So Garcia is finally going to make his move."

"Yep, and you can collar the bastard for us."

"Yeah...maybe." Tiredly Kit ran her fingers through her short black hair. Her voice trailed off into a quavering whisper. "Maybe..."

Chuck produced a severe frown. "All right, get your rear over to CG Headquarters at the Port of Miami. There's a Lieutenant Noah Trayhern who's expecting you."

The name sounded familiar, Kit mused. "Right now?" she asked, turning her attention back to Chuck.

Chuck consulted the watch on his thick wrist. "It's 10:00 a.m. Go clean out your locker. Lieutenant Trayhern requested you meet him at noon."

Kit shook her head morosely. She was twenty-eight going on eighty and feeling every minute of it. Releasing a long breath, she waved the papers that still needed to be signed at Chuck.

"Okay. Or should I practice saying aye, aye, sir?"

"That's my girl. You'll be okay, honey. Stay in touch?"

A genuine smile crossed her lips. "You're in my heart forever, Chuck. You know that."

"Ha! The man who gets your heart is going to be a lucky guy."

Kit grimaced, slowly pulling the leather strap of her purse across her slumped shoulder. "The only men interested in me are pimps who'd like to see me out on the street working for them when I'm undercover as a hooker. No thanks."

As she made her way down the noisy, crowded hall toward the locker rooms in the basement, Kit felt as if one heavy stone had been lifted off her and another put in its place. The narc division was filled with police officers who had learned to be actors and actresses. They could play the part of dope peddler, junkie or pimp to infiltrate organized crime in Dade County. Kit herself had become an actress for much larger stakes: she had posed as a rich Colombian landowner's daughter interested in connecting with the top of the drug hierarchy in southern Florida. She had been perfect for the part with her black hair, flawless Spanish and deep tan. She had lied and said her mother was American to explain her gray eyes. And because of her bravado, skill and courage, she had been able to infiltrate Jose Garcia's drug empire in Colombia. The information she'd gathered had dealt Garcia an almost lethal blow to his million dollar business. And the damage she'd caused them had cost the Mob stateside even more in drug sales. Yes, she had fooled them all and managed, thus far, to stay alive.

Kit found little in her locker worth retrieving. As she emptied the last of its contents, she dug out the address of the CG station. *Lieutenant Noah Trayhern,* she repeated to herself. Where had she heard that name before?

"I hope you don't have any bones to pick with me, Lieutenant Trayhern," she whispered softly, "because I'm down and out."

Something prompted Noah Trayhern to raise his head. The cubicle that served as his office sat opposite the entrance, and he looked up and saw a tall young woman standing just inside the main doors of the Coast Guard station. There was a decided air of loneliness around her that seemed to wear like a coat of armor, he thought, his green eyes narrowing in inspection. And her ill-fitting beige blazer over a plain white blouse and blue jeans indicated some carelessness about appearance.

Noah's gaze moved to her face, seeking a redeeming quality to counteract her initial image. Her eyes were large and expressive but held no life. They were slate gray and weary looking, with dark telltale shadows beneath them. Her finely sculpted chin held tension, warning him that although she might appear vulnerable, she had a stubborn streak. She was also underweight for her height, Noah observed, her cheeks hollow beneath her high cheekbones. Now his gaze was drawn to her mouth. She had beautifully formed lips that, despite her tension, pulled upward. That was good. It was her saving grace, Noah decided.

She was on guard, her feet planted slightly apart— a fighter's stance that Noah recognized. He, too, knew the value of keeping balance in devastating situations.

Kit noted the Coast Guard officer's appraisal and bridled inwardly as his impassive green eyes roved the length of her. But she coolly did a similar stocktaking of this tall, obviously athletic man. There was something about him that suggested calm, she decided. In fact, as she looked around, Kit began to register that the difference between the military headquarters and the police station was shocking. The noise level here was almost nonexistent. People working at nearby desks were actually smiling and joking with one another. And the smell was antiseptic clean, with a touch of ocean breeze to make it worth inhaling deeply.

"You're looking for someone," the officer said from the desk where he sat. "May I help you?"

Kit regarded him with growing interest. This man's well-modulated voice would soothe even the most violent junkie. Her stomach slowly began to unknot. And his sea-green eyes revealed a keen vitality with undeniable sparks of intelligence. Humor lurked at the corners of his well-shaped mouth—a mouth that looked accustomed to giving orders and having them carried out. Kit swallowed dryly, unable to break eye contact.

She moved closer to the desk. "I'm Detective Kit Anderson. I was told to be here by noon to meet a Lieutenant Trayhern."

Noah swallowed his shock as he stared up at her. A *woman* was being assigned to him? He sat for several seconds, digesting his surprise and anger. His commanding officer had told him that a police officer who could identify Garcia would be assigned to his cutter.

Noah had leaped at the opportunity. Anything to re-trieve his family's honor over his brother Morgan's tragedy. He rose hesitantly, bitterness coating his throat. The writing was too clearly on the wall: once again his superiors were going to try to railroad his career. This time they were handing him a woman agent to work with. She didn't appear capable of much. She looked more like a bedraggled stray in need of some care. She couldn't possibly be an undercover narc—one savvy enough to know Garcia. It must be a trick. An ugly calling card to remind him that the military hadn't forgotten about his brother.

Forcing his hand across the desk, he muttered, "I'm Noah Trayhern."

Automatically Kit placed her hand within his. The contrast was startling as her cold, damp hand disap-peared in his warm clasp. For a moment she felt the latent power in his grip, then she disengaged her hand, puzzled at the sudden sense of loss she felt. She'd watched surprise, anger and then a sullen look enter his assessing eyes. Confused, she took an aggressive stance in an attempt to protect her weary emotions.

"Why noon, Lieutenant? I barely had time to clean out my locker and—"

Scowling, Noah threw the report back on the desk. Right now he wanted to wrap his hands around his commander's throat. "I thought we might get ac-quainted over lunch," he muttered. *A woman, of all things.* He'd just been given one of the finest boats the Coast Guard had to command. And now his hopes of distinguishing his career for the honor of his family name were going to be sabotaged once again.

"Lunch?" Kit stalled, disconcerted by his apparent anger.

He tossed her a sharpened look. "It's the meal between breakfast and dinner. What's the matter? Don't the people over in narcotics ever see the light of day?"

Although she managed to remain impassive on the outside, Kit flinched internally when he opened and shut a desk drawer with force. His anger was directed at her. With a sinking feeling she realized that he didn't want a woman on the job with him. There was so little strength left in her, but Kit dredged up shreds of it, standing her ground. The kindness she'd seen in his face earlier had disappeared, and her heart cried out at the unfairness of the situation. "Look... Lieutenant, I don't like this any more than you do." Kit tried to make her voice sound firm and strong. "And I can see you're upset."

Noah glanced up after putting away the report and the pen. There was a pleading tone to her husky voice and in her eyes. Frowning, he nodded. "'Upset' isn't the word for it," he ground out. He felt the barely leashed tension within her; she was a mine ready to detonate. Noah tucked the observation away and held up his hands in a peacemaking gesture. "Okay—truce, Detective Anderson. You look pretty beat, and I've been up all night on a drug bust. I'm tired, but I'll try to be more responsible for my actions and less the little boy. Deal?"

"It's better than the alternative," she muttered. When he smiled, Kit felt as if the sun had come out again. Even if it was a grudging smile. Even if he was forcing it for her benefit. Still, her heart sank at the knowledge that he didn't want her around. Well, she didn't want him, either, she thought grimly. A year with this officer was likely to put her right over the edge.

Struggling to maintain an air of neutrality, Noah nodded. So many emotions were rising within him. Anger at the continued harassment by the Coast Guard was primary. But this woman officer was behaving like a prickly cactus, too. Shoving his reactions back down inside, Noah forced himself to be civil. He knew if he went to his superior and asked for the woman to be replaced, it wouldn't work. Whether he liked it or not he was stuck with her. Somehow, as he had on the other messy assignments he'd been given in the past, he'd have to make the best of it. Judging by the wariness still in her huge gray eyes, she hadn't sensed his decision.

"Let's start over," Noah suggested.

Was he really trying to make amends? Or was this a sham? Kit stared at him hard, allowing her instincts to take over. How long had it been since she'd spoken with a man who had such ease of bearing? There was no doubt he was a leader. And right now she felt the overwhelming urge to lean on someone stronger. Her senses told her Noah was such a man. Kit nodded. "Yes, let's start over. But why lunch?"

"Narc agents are shadow people. You sleep during the day and work all night. I figured you probably hadn't been out to lunch in a long time."

"I'm not really hungry, Lieutenant Trayhern, but if you are, let's go."

"Okay." Noah wanted to dislike her, but there was something ethereal about Kit Anderson that tugged hard at his heart. His emotions were automatically reaching out to her, but his mind was in turmoil about what to do with the situation in general. He wasn't going to have his career scuttled by this police detective. He intended to find Garcia. It would help his career and, perhaps, begin to remove the stain from his family name.

He moved around the desk, walking toward the doors. He stopped at the entrance and picked up his cap, hanging from a peg. She walked hesitantly at his side, and he could feel her withdrawal. Settling the cap on his head, he briskly opened the door for her, and they stepped out into the brilliant sunshine. "Do you mind if I call you Kit? It's less formal than Detective Anderson."

Startled, Kit retreated. His demeanor was suddenly warm, almost as if he'd never had his earlier negative reaction. Her mind went blank.

"Do you mind?" he repeated quietly.

"N-no... of course not."

Ignoring her stammer, he placed his hand on her elbow, guiding her down the walk and toward the parking lot at the rear of the building. "Call me Noah."

"I can't do that, Lieutenant," Kit replied tensely. His fingers were firm on her elbow. The desire to lean against him for just a moment was almost overpowering.

He gave her an amused glance as they left the walk and headed toward the rows of parked vehicles. "Sure you can."

Her lips thinned. She jerked her elbow from his hand, pulling to a halt. "This isn't a date we're going on, Lieutenant. I was assigned to DEA to interface between narc and the Coast Guard. You're my boss."

Noah threw his hands on his hips. Damn, but she was a contrary person! "That's right, I am. And a little civility is in order. You've been in those trenches too long."

Stung, Kit glared up at him. Her stomach began to knot again. "Now look, Trayhern, you can cut out the flirting act right now. I've got five tough years behind me in that drug jungle they call Dade County. I handled it, and I can handle you and this new assignment they threw at me. Keep your distance, be professional, and we'll get along."

Cocking his head, Noah studied her, gauging the fervent tone of her voice. The fire in her gray eyes interested him. "You think I'm flirting with you?" Her quicksilver temper intrigued him, and he liked her boldness and honesty. Of course professional conduct must rule. For just a moment he sensed the potential danger in letting himself think of Kit Anderson as a woman.

Kit gave him a flat look. "If the shoe fits, wear it."

"You are attractive," Noah admitted, "but I didn't ask to call you by your first name because I was flirting."

She watched him wearily. "We might as well get the rest of this settled right now."

"What else is eating at you?"

"Not me. You. I'm a woman being dropped into a 'man's job,' and I don't want to put up with chauvinism from you or your crew. I'm a police officer, Lieutenant Trayhern. A damn good one. You give me orders and I'll carry them out—or die trying. It makes no difference whether I'm male or female—I'll do the job for you."

Anger lurked beneath the surface in Noah and it came out in his voice. "You always spit bullets, Anderson?"

"Only when I'm fired upon."

"Are you always this tough?"

"When I have to be."

"I'm trying to patch things up between us, and you keep insisting on destroying my attempts."

Kit resisted the warmth in his eyes. She set her jaw, flashing him a dark look. "Then be honest. You didn't expect a woman on this assignment."

"Hell, no, I didn't!" Noah compressed his lips into a single line. "I got a file with 'K. Anderson' on the label. I assumed you were a man." He searched her upturned face. He was a good judge of people, and he sensed she was emotionally exhausted, though she kept it well hidden. "When your superior, Cordeman, called earlier, all he said was that you had one hell of an impressive record. He neglected to tell me you were a woman."

Touching her brow, Kit struggled with the rawness she felt. "Look, there's no way out of this assignment for us," she muttered. "If I could, I'd go back to Chuck Cordeman and ask for a transfer. But I'm the only one who can identify Jose Garcia." She raised her eyes, holding his hard stare. "Whether you like it or not, I'm here to stay. Maybe you can request a change of orders. Maybe there's another cutter captain who'd have less hostility about working with a woman."

Noah took off his hat, running his fingers through his military-short black hair. He settled the cap back on his head. "I wish the hell I could," he growled, glancing down at her. "But I'm just as stuck in this assignment as you are." If he requested a change because he didn't want to work with a woman, his career would be down the drain, and he knew it. "We're both going to have to bite the bullet on this one, Detective."

"Okay." Kit closed her eyes, feeling dizziness overwhelm her momentarily. She placed her feet slightly apart to steady herself. Chuck had thought this would be a plush, easy assignment. He'd been wrong. She didn't have the strength to be hard and tough with Noah Trayhern. That was an act she put on when undercover. In real life she wasn't anything like that. In real life the trauma of her undercover life had brought her close to an emotional breakdown. Kit knew she needed time to heal, but Lieutenant Trayhern wasn't going to give it to her. He was looking at her as if she were a noose around his neck.

"Come on," Noah muttered, "let's go to lunch."

"You're hungry?"

"No. But I need a drink."

Chapter Two

Kit felt more at ease in the darkened surroundings of the restaurant with Noah at her left elbow. She gave him a curious look after he ordered his drink.

"Did you purposely choose a corner where we could sit with our backs against the wall?"

"No. Why?"

"It's a good defensive position."

Noah gave her a keen look. "I see your back's to the wall. Do you find that preferable?"

"Of course," she confirmed. "Walls can't sneak up behind you and slide a knife between your ribs or fire at you when you aren't looking." Kit noticed Noah's hands. His fingers were long and capable looking. She could imagine him at the helm of a tall, four-masted sailing ship instead of a modern-day Coast Guard cutter.

"Why don't you just sit back and relax instead of eyeballing everyone who walks through that door? This is a restaurant, not a dive where drugs are being exchanged under the table."

"I've survived five years because I'm alert, Lieutenant. I'm not about to drop my guard just because you're with me."

Noah clamped down on a rejoinder. The waitress delivered his drink and Kit's large glass of milk.

Kit took a gulp of it, hoping it would quell her screaming stomach.

"Milk?" Noah goaded, eyeing the glass she clutched between her hands.

"Why not?" Kit asked defensively. "Do you have a problem with me drinking milk instead of liquor?"

Noah's mouth tightened momentarily as he held her stare. "No. But it could mean you have stomach ulcers. Do you?"

Her composure ruffled as Noah's open expression suddenly slid beneath an unreadable mask. It shook Kit, and her street instincts took over. Here was a man who could be generous, she suspected. Yet he wasn't to be trifled with, her gut warned. "It doesn't matter why I drink milk, Lieutenant. As long as I do my job, you shouldn't care what I eat, drink or do within reasonable limits."

Noah gave her a cutting smile. "Look, Detective Anderson, I don't know how Chuck Cordeman treated you, but I consider the people aboard the cutter my extended family. I try to treat each person the way I would want to be treated.''

"So far that quaint rule of conduct doesn't apply to me, does it?''

He throttled his mounting anger toward her. Noah knew she was right. "I'm applying it right now. I'm concerned about the state of your health.''

Kit shook her head. "My drinking milk isn't the real issue. Since when does an officer get friendly with the people beneath him? You and I both know there's a forbidden zone there. The military has a hierarchy just like the one over at the police department.''

"You do have a perverse attitude, don't you?'' Noah ground out.

Kit glared at him. "And you really get under my skin, Lieutenant.'' She took another swallow of the soothing milk. Licking her lips, she continued. "I've never met anyone like you in my entire life, and I've met some real winners.''

In that instant Noah saw her tough street mask slip. "Do you ever smile?'' he asked suddenly.

Kit jerked her head up. "What?''

Noah gave her a calculating look. "What the hell have they done to you, Kit, to make you so damned paranoid?''

The words, holding a hint of genuine tenderness, drove deeply into Kit's walled, aching heart. She blinked once, feeling the rush of hot tears. Noah's concerned face blurred before her. This time he wasn't acting. This was the real man beneath the hardened facade of the officer. *Care* was a foreign word to her.

No one cared for her but herself. Her lips parted in response and she sat frozen beneath his searching gaze, suddenly overwhelmed by the human side of Noah Trayhern. Bowing her head, she fought against the tears, willing them away.

"No you don't," he growled, gently capturing her nearest hand and placing a handkerchief in it. "It's not a crime to cry, you know."

Kit shoved the handkerchief back across the table. "I'm not going to break down like some soap opera character. Women don't always cry at the drop of a hat."

"I'm not going to answer your sarcasm, Kit. How long has it been since you last cried?"

Her eyes clouded with pain as she looked up at him. "Stop it!" she whispered, wanting to escape. At the tenderness burning in his eyes she rasped, "Cut the pity. There's nothing wrong with me!"

"Care is not pity," Noah grated out. He sat back grimly, watching her struggle with the deluge of emotions he'd unwittingly triggered in her. Stunned that he was drawn to her, he could say nothing. Kit Anderson touched him on so many levels that words escaped him, and silence hovered heavily between them.

Kit found it sheer agony to sit through lunch with Noah Trayhern. She ate little, her fingers visibly trembling as she lifted the glass to finish her milk. Occasionally she would catch him staring at her, sadness evident in his green eyes. Finally she could stand it no longer. After the waitress had cleared away the dishes, Kit placed both hands on the table and faced him squarely.

"Look, Lieutenant Trayhern, I know you must think I'm some kind of—"

"First," he interrupted sharply, "you're a woman, something the narc division conveniently overlooked. They've used you up and abused your qualities. You've been sucked dry emotionally." Noah's mouth became grim as he held her embarrassed gray eyes. "I'm not the new boy on the block when it comes to the drug world," he reminded her tersely. "I've been up to my neck in it since 1970. I'm one of two skippers who command the Bell Halter Surface Effect Ship. I interface with Drug Enforcement Agency headquarters, DEA agents in South America, the FBI, the CIA and local authorities to help halt drug trafficking. I've seen a hell of a lot of agents come and go in the past five years, and I know the narc type. I also know what working this dirty business has done to them." His voice deepened. "You've got ulcers, your hands tremble and you expect danger when there's nothing to fear."

Kit sucked in a sharp breath, feeling as if he'd glimpsed secret places in her that no one else suspected. Shakily she started to rise, but Trayhern gripped her arm, and she sank back down again.

"No," he ordered quietly. "First things first." His green eyes bore into hers. "You're taking a week off, Kit. Go home and get some sleep. And I mean deep, uninterrupted sleep. Lie in the sun. Learn how to relax. Consider this a minivacation in order to pull yourself back together again.''

She sat stiffly, unable to speak. Who was this man? He'd just probed her from top to bottom and discovered a truth she'd been avoiding for a long time. Drawing in a ragged breath, Kit became achingly aware of him as he released the grip on her arm. ''And then?'' she rasped, looking up into his face. Noah's eyes glittered with anger and a frown creased his forehead. He was angry with her, she thought in confusion, and disappointed.

''I'll call you sometime next week and we'll go over the details of your new job. We'll begin your integration into my unit slowly, provided we're given the time.''

''I've never failed any assignment I've undertaken.''

His mouth tightened, as if he were experiencing her pain. ''That's not what's at stake here, Kit,'' he countered less harshly.

''Then what is?''

Noah's eyes softened momentarily. ''You.'' He got to his feet. ''Come on,'' he coaxed, ''I'm taking you home. You need the rest.'' And then he added to himself, *I need time to think this thing through.* Maybe when he got back to the office, he could objectively evaluate Kit Anderson, her role and their assignment with each other. Like it or not, Noah had to acknowledge how powerfully he was drawn to her.

* * *

Noah had no sooner gotten back to his desk at headquarters than the phone rang. Muttering an oath under his breath, he picked it up.

"Coast Guard Headquarters, Lieutenant Trayhern speaking."

"Noah?"

He sat down. "Aly?" It was his younger sister, Alyssa, and she sounded depressed.

"I'm sorry to call you at work, Noah, but I just needed to hear a friendly voice."

"I know what you mean."

"Thank God for our family," Aly said fervently.

"Yeah," Noah agreed. The Trayherns were as tight as a family could get. They had to be. Since the events of 1970, Noah had watched his own blossoming military career go sour. Alyssa, who'd just entered the naval academy in 1970, had been given the silent treatment. Now she was in flight school at Pensacola, in northwestern Florida. "So how's it going, ace? Are you flying the wings off those planes up there?"

Aly's voice was low. "I'm trying to, Noah."

He gripped the phone a little tighter. "Pretty bad?"

"Yeah, really bad. God, Noah, I'm getting the silent treatment from the students all over again. I've got one instructor who does nothing but scream at me for an hour in the cockpit. He's trying to wash me out, make me quit. I—I don't know if I can hold it together...."

His throat tightened. "Hang in there, Aly. The Trayherns are made of tough stuff. We've got a two-hundred-year family military tradition to uphold. There's too much riding on both our shoulders to let go of that honor.''

"I'm getting tired, Noah. And I didn't want to tell Mom or Dad what's happening here at Pensacola. They worry too much about us, anyway.''

Noah tried to smile. "I'm glad you called. Any chance you might cut free for a weekend soon and visit me? Getting away from the name-calling and stares might help.''

"That would be wonderful, Noah. I really need a break. And I know Mom and Dad would die if they saw me right now. You know how they expect a monthly visit from each of us. I have dark circles under my eyes and I've lost a lot of weight since starting the flight program. These instructors really want me out, Noah. They want to disgrace me in retaliation for Morgan.''

"I know," he said softly, hurting for her. "Look, you get down here at the first opportunity, okay? My house has two guest bedrooms, and one of them has your name on it.''

Alyssa's tone was strained. "Thanks, big brother. I owe you one. I'll drop in to see you just as soon as I can.''

"Do that, Aly.''

"How are things with you? Are they still putting pressure on you?''

Noah managed a choked laugh. "Yeah, same old stuff.'' And then he told her about Detective Anderson and his latest assignment.

"Maybe this week off will get her in shape to be an asset instead of a problem for you," Aly offered.

Rubbing his face, Noah said, "God, I hope so. If she screws up, my career will be torpedoed. I fought so damned hard to get this SES billet. And now I've got a woman with a chip on her shoulder toward men."

"Just turn on some of that famous Noah Trayhern charm and she'll come around. I know she will."

He closed his eyes, buoyed by Aly's teasing warmth. "I hope you're right. I'm going over to her house on Friday and lay out the basic assignment to her."

"She'll be fine by then."

"Oh? You a psychic now?" he asked, chuckling.

"I've got a good feeling about her, Noah. Don't know why, but I just do. You'll know Friday for sure...."

There was no answer at Kit Anderson's bungalow door. Noah stood and listened, then rang the bell again. He'd tried to call earlier, but there'd been no response. Walking around the stucco one-story home, he spotted a high-walled wooden fence. Maybe she was in back, getting that suntan. Taking a chance, he opened the gate and moved quietly inside the closure.

Over the past few days Noah had tried to reconcile himself to the fact that Kit Anderson was going to be a part of his hardworking crew. Although still unconvinced that assigning a woman to this project was a good idea, Noah realized he'd treated her poorly upon first meeting her, and owed her an apology. Getting off on the wrong foot was no help to either of them.

Gazing across the lawn, he spotted Kit in a lavender bathing suit, lying on a chaise lounge. His hand tightened automatically around the briefcase he carried.

The late-morning sun had lulled Kit into a twilight of peace. Fragrant oleanders ringed the yard, scenting the late-morning air. Idly she ran her fingers across her lower arm, amazed at how deeply tanned she had become. Closing her eyes again, Kit enjoyed the call of the birds that made their homes in those ten-foot-high flowery bushes. In the years she had spent living at night, she'd missed their melodic songs.

Her languor ended at the sound of approaching footsteps. Instantly alert, Kit jerked into a sitting position, on guard. Noah Trayhern looked devastatingly handsome in his light blue shirt and dark blue slacks and garrison cap. He carried a briefcase in his left hand. Kit searched his face for signs of anger but saw none.

"I called earlier, but there wasn't any answer," Noah offered. "I thought I'd take a chance you might be back here." She looked slim and elegant in the revealing bathing suit. Puzzled as to why he hadn't realized how pretty Kit really was, Noah realized she was no longer in the baggy clothes that hid her innate femininity. His heart thudded hard in his chest, and he felt that familiar stirring that was beginning to seem inevitable whenever her name or face came to mind. And that had been often. Too damned often.

Kit lowered her lashes, hotly aware of a strange intensity to his inspection of her. She reached for her light blue beach jacket, quickly shrugging it across her shoulders. "It's better to get a tan in the morning," she said. Tying the sash, Kit stood. "I thought you'd conveniently forgotten about me."

Noah managed a crooked smile. "I had that coming, didn't I?"

Nervous beneath his continued stare, she crossed her arms. "Yes, you did."

"I'll try to change that."

Relief swept through Kit. There was something in his voice that said he was telling her the truth. "All I want to do is catch Garcia and survive this year with you, Lieutenant. I don't want any battles. I'm tired of fighting."

"I don't like to fight, either. Well," he amended, "only druggies. I didn't call you because I didn't want to disturb you."

Kit remained on guard. Noah was a man of incredible insight, and it unnerved her to suspect that he probably knew as much about her as she did herself. "If we've got business to discuss, come on in the house. I've got some sun tea made. Would you like a glass?"

"Sounds good. And yes, we've got business to discuss."

She nodded, seeing the undisguised hunger in his face. It rattled her badly. "I'm ready to work. I've had my fill of soap operas and crossword puzzles."

He walked easily beside her, and Kit admired his aura of confidence. It gave her a sense of stability when she had none left within herself. Somehow Noah

Trayhern made her feel safe. Right now she didn't want to probe the reasons why too deeply.

"You needed this time, though," Noah reminded her.

"Maybe," Kit hedged, walking into the cool interior of the small, neatly kept house. "The kitchen's that way," she instructed. "I'll change into something more appropriate and be out in a minute. Why don't you pour us some tea?"

Noah busied himself in the kitchen. When Kit emerged from the bedroom ten minutes later, she was dressed in a pair of pale pink shorts and a sleeveless blouse. Its pink-and-fuchsia print with burgundy accents highlighted her golden skin. He found it difficult not to stare. Picking up her glass of tea, he met her halfway.

"I like what you've done to your hair," he noted, handing her the cool glass. Their fingers met and touched.

Kit fingered the wispy bangs over her brow. She had coaxed her black hair into soft waves around her face. "Thank you," she muttered nervously, and took the glass, barely able to endure Noah's examination. Heat rushed into her face. My God, was she blushing? Touching her flaming cheek, Kit was at a loss for words.

Noah fought himself, but he lost out to the driving need to touch her. He placed his hand beneath her chin and gave her an approving look. "No circles under your eyes, either." Her flesh was soft and far too inviting. It was the shock in her eyes that forced him to drop his hand back to his side. He wasn't behaving professionally, and that irritated him. What was it about her that invited this kind of familiarity?

Kit's skin tingled where Noah's hand had fleetingly rested. Despite an initial hesitancy, she found herself responding to him like a flower parched for water, drawn helplessly to him. He seemed to put her in touch with her own vulnerability and restore the sense of femininity that had long been buried by her under-cover career.

"Come into the living room," she said, shaken. She took a chair opposite Noah. The coffee table acted as a barrier between them, allowing her to relax slightly. Clearing her throat, she said, "I still don't know what to make of you, Lieutenant."

Giving her a wry glance, he selected several groups of papers from his briefcase and spread them across the coffee table. "Call me Noah."

"Even in front of the DEA, FBI and CIA people?" Kit taunted. Every second spent with him was dissolving her barriers. Noah was too much like Pete, she admitted to herself. The Coast Guard officer appeared driven, probably a superachiever, just as her partner, Pete, had been. Noah reminded her too much of the recent past, but she had no way to stop his encroachment on her life, either professionally or, even more frightening, personally.

"Even with them," he agreed affably, hearing the disbelief in her voice. Glancing up, he said, "My crew and I work well together, Kit. They all know who's boss and we know our responsibilities. I came out of

a very tight-knit family myself, and I know the bene-
fits of one. I apply that same philosophy to my crew.''

She gave him a strange look. "Family?" His last
name struck a memory chord within her once again.

Noah looked up. "Why not?"

"Wait a minute..." Kit snapped her fingers, finally remembering where she'd heard his name. Her
eyes rounded. "My God, you aren't from *the* Trayhern family with the traitor, are you?" Kit saw Noah's
eyes go dark with hurt, then anger, and she instantly
regretted how she'd framed her question.

Noah's hands stilled over the reports spread before
him. He struggled with the grief and loss of Morgan,
and then the anger that she or anyone would dare call
his older brother a traitor. Kit was just one more person to parrot what she'd been fed by the press. She
hadn't grown up with Morgan, didn't know how loyal
he was or how much integrity he possessed. Wrestling
with an avalanche of stripped feelings, Noah whispered tautly, "Yes, Morgan is my brother." Funny, he
never could say was. He didn't accept that Morgan
was dead. He couldn't. And neither did anyone else in
his family.

Kit placed a hand across her mouth, the huskiness
in his voice tearing at her. "Oh, no..."

Noah misinterpreted her reaction as negative and
sighed roughly. "We might as well hash this out right
now." He tried to prepare himself for her outrage at
having to work with the brother of a supposed traitor. He'd gone through this scenario for five years
now. Would it never end?

"No... I mean, I'm sorry. It's just that the memory hit me so hard and out of nowhere," Kit blurted. She desperately wanted peace between them, not more dissension. Some of the hardness left his eyes, replaced with grief. Kit ached for him, realizing the pain he'd carried because of his infamous brother. "It must be awful to have endured the names and blame for something you didn't do."

Noah searched her flushed features, her eyes soft and dove gray. He'd expected anger and accusations from Kit. Instead she was desperately trying to mend the fence between them. His voice came out low and tortured. "First of all, my family and I don't consider Morgan a traitor. He was a captain in the Marine Corps in charge of a company of men in Vietnam. Something happened over there, and his entire company was wiped out, except for him and one other man."

Kit bit her lower lip, feeling the magnitude of his anguish. "Everything I read in the papers and saw on television said he deserted his men, leaving them to die. They said he deserted to North Vietnam—the other survivor swore he ran away."

Noah shook his head, as if trying to shake off an invisible millstone he carried. "Morgan would never desert anyone. Our family prides itself on taking care of those under us. He was raised to be loyal to a fault, and we feel he's been made a scapegoat for something that went wrong. My father, who was a general in the air force at the time, tried to investigate, but he was stopped at every turn. That's why we believe Morgan was somehow framed.'' Raising his chin, Noah caught and held her gaze. ''There's no way to prove it. Besides, it's the past, and we've got to work in the present.''

''I remember something about your family having a two-hundred-year military tradition. Every child of each generation went into one of the services.''

''That's right. In my generation, Morgan went into the Marine Corps. I went into the Coast Guard and our younger sister, Alyssa, went into the navy as a pilot. She's in flight training in Pensacola right now.''

Kit saw the pride in his eyes, heard the pride in his voice for his family and its name. ''If Morgan didn't desert, then your whole family must be bearing a terrible burden.''

''We've all paid for it in some way,'' he muttered, unwilling to discuss it any further. ''But I guess everyone has his or her personal set of problems to carry around.''

''Some have more than others,'' Kit said softly, overwhelmed at the immensity of Noah's load.

His eyes bore into hers. ''Is my family history going to be a problem between us?''

Shakily Kit rubbed her hands together, unable to meet his gaze. ''No,'' she whispered tightly, ''it won't. It just helps me understand you, that's all.''

Noah wanted to say, *Understand me how?* But he didn't. Kit looked genuinely apologetic for her outburst. Rallying because he believed her, he said, ''Come over here. Let's get this briefing over with.''

Slowly Kit rose. There was a dangerous edge to Noah Trayhern that triggered the flight mechanism within her. She sat down on the couch, far enough away to avoid any direct bodily contact. But she was less nervous now that she realized that she and Noah shared similar unhappy, gut-wrenching pasts. Pete had abandoned her. Morgan had abandoned his family. She had paid for Pete's supercop heroics, and Noah had paid for his brother's horrifying mistake.

Noah pulled out an eight-by-ten black-and-white photograph and handed it to her. "This is our ship, the *Osprey*. It's an SES."

Kit studied the photo, admiring the clean, sleek lines of the Coast Guard cutter. "She's beautiful." In an effort to lighten the atmosphere, Kit added teasingly, "I assume you still refer to ships as 'she'?"

He rallied beneath her obvious attempt to smooth things out between them. There was an endearing quality to Kit, Noah decided sourly. And it wasn't helping him maintain his professional demeanor with her. "The day any ship quits behaving like a fickle, beautiful woman is the day I'll start calling it 'he,'" Noah admitted. "The *Osprey* will be your home for one to seven days at a time. We have cramped crew quarters, a galley and all the social amenities packed into a small space. Quite a bit of room is reserved for the boarding crews, rifles, ammunition. There's also a hold for the storage of confiscated drugs."

Kit's eyes grew large. "Seven days?" She'd never set foot on a boat in her life.

"Most of the time it's one-day missions, five days a week. But we're going to be hunting for Garcia, so our trips will be longer in order to be in his backyard when he decides to do business with the smugglers. We'll be off the coast of South America or in the Gulf of Mexico from time to time because of our assignment."

Kit grimaced. "Chuck was right—I'll turn into a sailor."

"It's better than being a narc patrolling back alleys."

Sobering, Kit muttered, "You're right, I suppose." She tried to shake off the gloom of five years in the trenches and Pete's desertion. "I've never been out to sea, Noah," she warned him, unease plain on her face.

It was the first time she'd called him by his first name. Noah relaxed slightly. Maybe, with time, Kit would call a truce between them and they could both quit carrying a chip on their shoulders. "We've got Dramamine aboard," he reassured her. "I'll let you in on a little secret, though."

"What?"

"Even the crew gets seasick sometimes. It gets pretty rough out in the Gulf and Caribbean at certain times of year. So you'll be in good company."

"This is like an unfolding nightmare. I'm a land-lubber. And I'm not a great swimmer, either."

"I'll give you a tour of the *Osprey* and maybe that

will help.'' He handed her a report. ''You're going to have to learn what we do and where you fit into the scheme of things. Let's get down to the business at hand.''

Chapter Three

How can I concentrate? Kit wondered distractedly. She tried to remain objective as the briefing continued, but Noah's presence sabotaged her attempts. Pete had been dead a little less than a year now, and Kit was painfully aware of how much she missed having a man in her life. Not that she and Pete had been lovers. No, it had been strictly professional—but undeniably personal. They'd been an unbeatable team on the streets until...

Kit tried to squelch the horrible images that rose in front of her. She shut her eyes tightly, trying to control the sudden surge of grief and loss.

"Here's the map of the territory we have to patrol," Noah pointed out, interrupting her thoughts.

He placed the chart before them on the coffee table, using his index finger to trace the areas of activity. "There are four major choke points where Garcia might appear. These are also where we tend to intercept most of the drugs en route to the United States. We've got the Yucatán Channel, the Windward Passage, the Mona Passage and the Anegada Passage."

Kit managed to surface from the mire of grief. "What happens at those points?"

"Our chances of intercepting Garcia in a sixty- to two-hundred-foot class of mother ship are much greater." Noah rested his strong chin on his clasped hands as he gazed over at her. "Mother ships carry the bales of marijuana, dropping them off by crane to small ships and boats that try to smuggle them into our waters. The Coast Guard plies 1.8 million square miles of open seas, but the DEA feels Garcia will show up at one of these choke points."

"And we'll be there?"

"Sometimes. It depends on weather conditions. It's May now, and beginning in August we're building toward hurricane season. No one knows when Garcia might make his move. We know it will be within a year, but not when."

"And you need me on board to identify the bastard, right?"

Noah watched her face grow tense. "Yes. We could end up catching him, then turning him loose without even being aware of who he is. You were the only agent to successfully infiltrate his organization in Colombia and can identify him on sight. That's pretty impressive when you consider Garcia can smell an agent ten miles away.''

Kit's breathing grew harsher, and she tried to control the hatred welling up inside her. Running her fingers agitatedly through her hair, she whispered, ''Don't get me started on him. He's the key man in all my nightmares.''

''It must have been rough on you.'' Instinctively Noah reached out and placed his hand on her arm in a gesture of comfort. Her skin was warm and smooth, sending an ache through him. There was something mysterious and primal about Kit that had nothing to do with her being a police detective. Noah had spent all week mulling over his unexpected attraction to her. She seemed unaware of her own sensuality. Yet he sensed it—still, powerful and profound. Reluctantly he released her arm and focused his attention back on business.

Shaken by the sudden intimacy Noah had established with her, Kit retreated inside herself—the only place of real safety she knew. ''Garcia's rough on everyone.''

''No argument from me. We've been wanting him a long time. The DEA is calling this 'Operation Storm,' because Garcia will, in all likelihood, take his mother ship out during hurricane season. But we can't be sure. That's why we need you with us on every bust. Only you've survived to make a positive ID. The only other person who knows his real identity is his accomplice, Emilio Dante.''

Kit's mouth thinned. "Him," she stated flatly, a cold shiver moving up her back.

Noah nodded grimly. Garcia was known for his cold-blooded murders of agents who had tried over the years to infiltrate his vast drug empire in Colombia. Kit had been the only agent to successfully accomplish it and live to tell about it.

Lady, you're very special. And how I admire your courage, Noah thought, glancing over at her bent head. But her bravery had taken a terrible toll on her, and Noah sensed her fragile hold on her emotions. "You can read the report on Operation Storm between today and tomorrow. If you're not doing anything tomorrow afternoon, I'll take you over to the *Osprey* and you can get acquainted with the ship."

"I'll warn you right now, Noah, I don't care for boats." Kit tried to appear calm despite the adrenaline pumping through her. When Noah had touched her, she had wanted to melt into his arms. But her attraction to him wasn't clear or simple. In fact, she wasn't at all comfortable with these newly emerging feelings. Who was he, anyway? In her undercover work she met only the worst of men. Noah seemed like a knight in shining armor by contrast, incorporating Pete's driven quality with a special underlying gentleness. How could she fight this attraction and still do her job as a cop?

Resting his arms against his long, muscular thighs, Noah managed a slight smile. "I think you'll find the *Osprey* a solid vessel. Sometimes when we board the druggie boats, the action can get tight. More than one

member of our boarding party has been pushed overboard and had to be rescued.''

"I guess it can't be more dangerous than Dade
County," Kit ventured wryly.

"On a small, cramped boat there's no place to hide
from bullets," Noah warned, his brows dipping.
"You'll be the DEA representative aboard our ship.
We have radio com-nets with the Miami police, the air
force, navy, customs and other CG units. Since you
speak fluent Spanish, you can be our interpreter when
we need one. You'll also relay info to IOIC—Inter-
diction Operations Information Center—and help us
identify suspects as we pick them up off boats.''

"Then I'll be part of the boarding party?"

Noah firmly shoot his head. "No, you'll stay
aboard the *Osprey* until we've secured the boarding.
No rough stuff for you, lady.''

In a way Kit was relieved. For five years she'd
worked undercover without any kind of protection. If
she'd carried a pistol, she would have blown her cover
and been recognized as a cop. She'd lived by her wits
and her ability to survive. "Then all I'll need is my
shoulder revolver.''

"You won't need to carry one.''

Kit gawked at him. Was he crazy? She almost said
it but caught herself in time. "Look, you're painting
a pretty dangerous picture. I want to carry a revolver
on your ship, just in case.''

Noah gave her an unruffled look. "The only people who carry weapons on the *Osprey* are the boarding party. No one else has one. That's the rule.

Besides, I don't intend to have you close enough to the action to get shot at," he explained patiently.

"I hear male chauvinism talking, and I don't like it. I'm not some helpless female who—"

"You're under my command, Kit," he interrupted firmly. "I intend to make sure you'll be safe. My crew is specially trained for boarding procedures. You're along as liaison." Her gray eyes were glittering angrily and he tried to defuse the tension between them. "What's the matter, don't you think I'll keep my promise?"

"Experience has taught me to be leery of trusting men's promises, Noah. They're capable of breaking their word when it suits them."

Noah held on to his disintegrating patience. "As long as you're under my authority, you'll have to live with my orders. I'll make sure you're properly protected."

"I can take care of myself," Kit gritted out.

Moving his shoulders to release the accumulated tension, Noah said, "Can't any man or woman, up to a point?"

"Don't play word games with me!"

Noah slowly sized her up, realizing he was striking at the core of her stubbornness. "You're so damned independent that you don't know when to lean on someone for support."

Kit reared back as if struck. "That's your opinion, Lieutenant Trayhern. Just because I'm a woman doesn't make me less capable of surviving. I learned the hard way that a man can't even protect himself, much less me!''

She got up and turned angrily, then marched down the hall. Taking deep breaths, she walked out into the backyard to cool down. Not more than ten seconds passed before Kit heard the back door open and close. She turned, still trembling with anger, her arms belligerently crossed over her chest.

Noah Trayhern's features were thundercloud dark as he approached her. Kit tensed, uncrossing her arms, allowing her hands to drop to her sides as he halted inches from where she stood. His eyes were the color of a stormy sea as he appraised her in the icy seconds afterward.

''I swore I wouldn't let myself be affected by your negative attitudes,'' he began, his voice low with fury. ''But I am. For some reason, you don't trust men. And whoever caused that kind of damage to you ought to be hung out to dry.'' His voice became more coaxing. ''The only thing that will make our relationship bearable is total honesty. Don't project on me the images of previous men in your life.''

''I'm sorry, Noah,'' she offered, confusion in her gray eyes. ''You hit a sensitive chord in me. I shouldn't have overreacted like that.''

He hung his head and released a long sigh. ''I've tried to figure you out, Kit. You're a woman in a man's world as an undercover agent. That's a harsh kind of life for anyone, much less a sensitive person like you. Second, I think a man has damn near destroyed you emotionally in the past.'' He narrowed his eyes with concern. ''Am I right?''

Kit nodded painfully. ''Right on all counts.'' She turned away and went to the chaise lounge, sitting down. Noah followed and crouched beside her, sympathetically placing his hand on her knee. She accepted his gesture for what it was, and openly studied his face. It was generous and trusting, and Kit felt a desperate need to trust him right now. ''What are you, an amateur psychologist?'' she asked, attempting lightheartedness.

Noah took her hands and held them in his own. ''I think in our business it becomes second nature,'' he offered quietly. ''Level with me, will you?''

''Why?'' Just the warming touch of his strong, protective hands sent a burst of stability through her.

''Because I care.'' Far more than he should, Noah added inwardly. Far more than she would ever know. ''Is that reason enough?''

Kit looked up guardedly. Her heart ached, and need finally won out over her fear. ''Okay, what do you want to know?''

The grip of his fingers tightened momentarily. ''Who made you so distrustful of men?''

Fighting a deluge of emotions, she stammered, ''Is—is this necessary, Noah?''

''Kit, we're going to be working closely together,'' he explained, his eyes never leaving her taut features, ''and I need to know your strengths and weaknesses, just as you'll know mine.''

She searched his face. Her heart thrashed about like a bird caught in a trap. Pain began to ebb from that tightly walled chamber. Kit withdrew her hands and buried her face in them. She felt Noah's reassuring hand sliding across her shoulders in a gesture of support.

A ragged breath escaped her lips, and she lifted her chin, staring blindly past Noah. "I'm sure my personnel file shows that Pete Collins was my partner for four years out of the last five."

Noah searched his mind; he'd read her file thoroughly, committing it to memory. "It does."

She gulped unsteadily. "The last three generations of my family have been police officers. I have three older brothers and they were already police graduates. I followed that family tradition. Except I had all those pie-in-the-sky dreams about helping people."

"You were a supercop with a high degree of patriotism, and you wanted to strike at the roots of one of our worst problems."

Kit winced and nodded miserably. "Supercop. You hit the nail on the head . . ." Gathering her courage to go on, Kit continued in a strained tone. "When I graduated and demanded narc duty, Chuck Cordeman gave me Pete Collins for a partner. He was a supercop, too. Only he had ten years experience and all kinds of commendations. He was a hotshot, just like you are. As an impressionable twenty-three-year-old, I emulated him in almost every way."

"Your file shows four years of impressive collars, Kit. And you've got a lot of commendations."

Sadness overwhelmed her. "My father's proud of me. That's all that counts."

Noah understood what she meant. All his life he'd striven to live up to the glorious thirty-year military career that had won his father, Chase Trayhern, nearly every conceivable medal. "You said you emulated Pete."

"Not quite." Kit's voice turned harsh with agony. "Pete had a family—a lovely wife and two kids. He had me as his backup and partner. He had everything, Noah, but he threw it all away."

"What do you mean?"

"His wife divorced him the second year I was with him because he took too many chances. We were always mixing it up with the Mob collars, and there were a lot of shots fired. Finally Valerie couldn't stand his John Wayne tactics, and she took the children back to California. She couldn't live in the constant fear of him dying." Kit rubbed her aching brow. "I tried to tell Pete he should have cared more for them, for his wife and kids. But he just kept taking chances...."

Grimly Noah looked at her. "He was taking constant chances with your life, too," he suggested softly.

"Yeah...I guess he was...." She closed her eyes. "But I was too naive to know that at the time. I was so caught up in the image he presented that I was like his shadow. And I was too inexperienced to see that he was a heavy drug user himself."

Noah frowned, his grip tightening on her shoulder. "Hard drugs?"

"Yeah." Kit laughed hollowly. "I was so intent upon cleaning up the streets of Miami that I failed to see Pete and his problem! God, how could I have been so blind?"

"We're all blind at some point in our lives. So when did you discover his habit?"

"It was just a few months before he died. Pete's bravado and risk taking were sort of a death wish. The thing he hated most in the world had control over his life. When I put two and two together, I tried to talk to him about it."

"And?"

Kit shook her head, giving Noah a grief-stricken look. "When I confronted him with it, he denied it."

"Typical of a junkie."

Kit valiantly tried to stem the rising tide of anguish that threatened to shut off her breathing. "Typical," she croaked.

"You're doing fine. What happened next?"

Her shoulders dropped, and her eyes remained fixed on him. "Those months were hell," she rasped. "Once Pete knew I was aware of his drug problem, he didn't care what he did. He just kept taking stupid chances."

"Were you emotionally involved with him?"

"If you're asking if we were lovers, the answer is no. I was emotionally involved from the standpoint that he was my partner. He'd been like a hero to me, and we'd spent too many years together not to have feelings of intense loyalty."

Noah studied her tortured features. At a gut level he sensed that Kit *had* been in love with Pete Collins. Had she been naive about love before meeting the larger-than-life supercop? If so, then Pete Collins could have had an almost mesmerizing effect on Kit and her young, untutored emotions.

"Was he like a father to you?" Noah asked, trying to put their relationship into some kind of focus.

"More like a big brother." She managed a sad smile. "He was wonderful, Noah. So proud, brave and strong. And then he became just like the filth we were busting."

Noah's stomach knotted. "Did he become violent with you?"

"Not physically. But brutality comes in many forms, Noah. You know that and so do I. Pete beat me down emotionally and mentally until I began losing it."

"So narc duty and your home life became one and the same?"

"I never had a home life. Narc was my life. I—I never could talk to Dad about this. I'm sure he'd have expected me to turn Pete in. I felt guilty about not being able to talk Pete into getting help. I was walking a tightrope with Pete in the middle of the Garcia undercover operation. I posed as a Colombian, and Pete was my older brother who handled things stateside."

"I remember reading in the paper how Emilio Dante was collared. You were responsible for that, weren't you?"

A shudder worked up her spine, and Kit hid her face in her hands to hide the emotions etched on it. "Dante was Garcia's main man. I lured Dante to Miami for capture. At the last moment, just before the bust went down, Pete took an unbelievably stupid chance and Dante gunned him down.''

Noah felt as if a fist had slammed into his heart. ''Right in front of you?''

''Y-yes. Damn Pete Collins!'' she sobbed. ''He should have cared more about his family, himself or even his partner, me! And he didn't! All he could do was grandstand, adding another commendation to his record and having the other cops look up to him. I really believe he was more afraid of them finding out he was a junkie than he was of getting killed.''

Her anguish scored his chest. She was trembling, and he guessed that she hadn't cried for a year. He wrapped his arm around her. ''I'm sorry,'' Noah soothed, ''I didn't mean to make you hurt this way. It's over, Kit. Just let go of the pain. I'll hold you...''

Noah's gentleness shattered her immobility. Fear vomited through Kit, and she tore out of his embrace with a cry. She saw the surprise on his features as he looked at her.

''Just leave me alone!'' she begged hoarsely. ''Just go away!'' Hanging on to the grief and tears, Kit whirled around, running for the safety of her house. Blindly she ran down the hall to her bedroom, closing the door behind her. With shaking hands, she locked it. Knees wobbly, she made it to the bed and curled in a tight ball, unable to release the past because Noah Trayhern reminded her too much of Pete Collins.

As she lay there, eyes tightly shut, Kit saw too many similarities between the two men. Only this time, Noah's gentleness and understanding had made her vulnerable in a way she'd never encountered. Pete had never been tender, much less sensitive to anyone but himself. But Noah had some of Pete's other attributes—a drive to be the best, to overcome a personal failing, although in Noah's case it was to compensate for his brother, Morgan. He was a supercop in a Coast Guard uniform.

Muffling a cry, Kit rolled onto her stomach, clutching a pillow, buried in a mire of past and present anguish. There was no way out, no answer. Somehow she'd have to stop the unraveling emotions that Noah had jerked free within her, and try to work with him. But where was she going to get the strength? And what would Noah do about her past? She'd trusted him enough to tell the truth. What would he do with that volatile information?

"Are you Chuck Cordeman?"

Cordeman raised his head from the mound of paperwork that seemed to attack him from every direction. "Yeah, I'm Cordeman. Who are you?" he shot back in an irritated tone. The noise surrounding them couldn't be blocked out, although the narc supervisor's office was enclosed by a sturdy glass panel. Phones were ringing constantly, and men and women in plainclothes with police IDs hanging on their shirts milled around in the larger outer office.

"I'm Lieutenant Noah Trayhern of the Coast Guard." Noah didn't offer his hand.

Leaning back in his lumpy chair, Cordeman studied him a moment. "Have a seat."

"We've got some business to discuss."

"Look, I'm pretty busy, Lieutenant. If you can make it quick I—"

"Stow it, Cordeman. What I've got to tell you isn't going to wait." Noah took a deep breath, trying to control his emotions. "I left Kit Anderson's house an hour ago."

Cordeman's bushy eyebrows drew into a heavy scowl. "So?"

Noah's expression hardened as he placed both hands flatly on Cordeman's desk, glaring down at the pudgy supervisor. "When I met Kit, I knew she was in bad shape. That's why I fought IOIC to give her a week's rest before we initiated Operation Storm." His nostrils flared. "She hasn't improved. Now you're going to throw your considerable departmental weight into this lopsided battle to help get her two or three more weeks of rest. She's not anywhere close to being ready to step into this damn snake pit of an operation!"

Cordeman glared up at him. "I think you'd better calm down!"

"You really don't care if Kit Anderson can survive this bust, do you?" Noah asked angrily.

Cordeman shot out of his chair and leaned across the dilapidated desk. "Now just one damn minute,

Trayhern! Who the hell do you think you are, coming in here with accusations like that?''

"I'm responsible for Kit Anderson," Noah countered. "She's officially part of my team, Cordeman. And *I* do care what happens to my people. Particularly when so much is at stake." His eyes narrowed to slits of fury. "You knew Kit was broken emotionally before you sent her to us, didn't you? You knew it, and sent her, anyway. Why did you do it, Cordeman?"

Cordeman's jaw jutted outward, and his face turned red. "Kit is a damn good agent!" he breathed. "The best! The captain wanted her on this operation because she's the only one who can identify Garcia. She's the only one to come back alive from his fortress. That's *why* she's been assigned to you, Trayhern. Is that clear enough?"

Noah dug his fingers into the desk, his knuckles whitening. "A lot of good her knowledge is going to serve if she's mentally and physically on the edge. You know that and so do I!"

Cordeman reared back, glowering at Noah. His raspy breathing heated up the silence lengthening between them. "Okay," he muttered. "So she's almost washed up. Kit will hold together for you. She's tough. She's got what it takes."

"She bought it less than a year ago, Cordeman! Kit's been running on raw nerves and ulcer medicine since then. Who the hell are you trying to fool?"

The narc supervisor's shoulders dropped. "Okay, okay," he groused, "so Kit's been going downhill for a while."

Noah straightened, his eyes blazing. "Kit lost her partner, Pete Collins. And you didn't even have the humanity to give her time to recover. You just pushed her back into the trenches, hoping she'd forget about it."

Cordeman's gaze moved to the floor. "Look, I feel badly about this. . . . Kit's like a daughter to me."

"No father in his right mind would have done what you did," Trayhern snarled. "She looked to you for support, Cordeman, and you ignored all the warning signs. I don't buy the father figure routine."

The older man sat heavily on his chair, not meeting Noah's eyes. "Kit was hysterical after Pete's death."

"Did you know he was hooked on drugs?"

Cordeman studied him harshly. "At the time, no. And if I had, I'd have hauled him off duty, taken his badge and sent him into rehabilitation. Kit kept that knowledge to herself and tried to help him, but she failed. What she did was wrong. She should have come to me. But she was too young and too loyal to Pete."

"So you found out after he died?"

"Yeah. I went over to the hospital and that's where she spilled the whole ugly story." He shook his head. "They had a special relationship, Trayhern. It wasn't love, but it was a commitment to each other to be the best at what they did. They were one hell of a team. Ever since Kit lost him, she's been sliding."

"So after Collins's death you sent her right back out there?"

Cordeman glared at him. "What else could I do?"

"You could have gotten her some therapy, for God's sake!" Noah spit out. "Emotionally, she was *never* cut out for narc duty, but she was trying to please her father, Collins and you." Noah grimaced, fury racing through him. "Kit Anderson shouldn't have been a cop. She hasn't got what it takes to deal with the brutality of it all. You've used up her strength, her spirit and her will to live. Right now, she's close to an emotional breakdown."

"So what the hell do you want me to do about it?"

"You side with me against IOIC and get Kit three more weeks of recuperation time before we initiate Storm."

"Three weeks?" he cried. "You're out of your mind!"

"Three weeks," Noah ground out, "or she'll be dead on this bust and we both know that." He rested his hands against the desk, hovering over the narc supervisor. "And I'm not going to allow that to happen, Cordeman. You hear me? Either you side with me, or I'll throw so many wrenches into this operation that you'll scream like a stuck hog. I know your captain is going up for promotion soon. And I suspect he's counting on Storm to make him look like a regular tin god in front of the good city fathers. I carry weight over at the CG. I'll screw your department so damn hard that your captain will bury you so deep you'll never see the light of day."

Cordeman's eyes grew round. "Do you know how hard it is to get something like that approved? The paperwork alone will weigh ten pounds!"

"I refuse to knowingly put one of my people's lives on the line. Kit is part of my team, Cordeman. Side with me or else. Her life is more important than any drug bust or captain's promotion."

Cordeman continued to glower at Noah, but his tone admitted defeat. "You've got balls, Trayhern."

"See that Kit gets those three weeks," Noah repeated grimly.

"If it will make you feel any better, I tried to get Kit off this assignment."

Noah was sure his eyes indicated his distrust. He had worked with Cordeman from a distance on several occasions in the past. He knew the man's reputation for integrity and an unwavering attitude toward drug smugglers. Cordeman also ran one of the toughest narc divisions in the country. He was good at his job and had a decided talent for getting the best out of the people who worked under him. Maybe a little too good, Noah decided. Kit had returned to work instead of taking time off to adjust to the death of her partner. "Just how hard did you try?"

Cordeman motioned him toward the chair. "Sit down," he growled, his blue eyes narrow. "You're gonna find out, Trayhern, that I do take a great deal of interest in my people." He paused as Noah sat. "I had plans to force Kit to take a leave of absence from the department before Operation Storm was created by DEA. I knew she was hurting, and I tried a number of times to persuade her to talk about it. But she wouldn't. She kept insisting she was all right. About six months ago, she began to make mistakes. It was little things, but she realized as well as any of us that in this business details can get you killed. Finally she came and asked me for a transfer out of the department."

Noah frowned. "Out of narc completely?"

"Yeah. Kit admitted to me that she'd had it. She wanted a desk job—anything to get her off the streets. I promised her I'd do my damnedest."

"With her record of commendations, it should have been easy," Noah pointed out tightly.

Cordeman met his glare. "I went straight to the captain with it. I told him she was at the end of the line emotionally and needed the rest. That was when he told me about Storm." He shook his head sadly. "You know how important Kit is to the success of this operation. If we can get Garcia out of the picture, the Colombian government will cooperate with us in prosecuting him. Garcia's smart—he stays out of the limelight. Anybody trying to take a photo of him can kiss his life goodbye."

Noah rubbed his jaw. "So what kind of deal did you wrangle for her?"

"A lateral transfer to your ship as a liaison observer."

"And after that?"

"After Storm's completed, Kit gets her wish. She gets a cushy desk job as a detective in homicide upstairs."

"Maybe I've misjudged you, Cordeman. And maybe I haven't."

The supervisor sank wearily back into his frayed leather chair. He mopped his brow with a limp white handkerchief. "I'll get Kit those three weeks. Somehow."

Rising, Noah muttered, "Call me as soon as it's official."

Chapter Four

Noah had barely gotten back to headquarters to finish up some paperwork, when Cordeman called. Sitting down at his desk, he took the call.

"Coast Guard. Lieutenant Trayhern speaking."

"This is Cordeman. I've got some bad news for Kit."

Automatically Noah placed a clamp on his emotions. "What's wrong?"

"Plenty. Emilio Dante was just released from prison. Kit was the one who put him away, Trayhern. And he swore that when he got out he'd settle the score with her. Well, he's out, and our snitch just told one of my undercover officers that he's planning to go after her."

Cold fear washed through Noah. "How in hell did that happen? Dante was supposed to be put away for fifteen years."

"His lawyers got him out on bail due to a technicality. There will be another trial. Until then, he's walking around free and vowing revenge. With him out, Operation Storm takes on new importance."

"That's the least of our problems," Noah shot back, irritated. His mind whirled with options on how to protect Kit. She'd have to go into hiding. She was a sitting duck at her home. His heartbeat quickened at the thought of Kit in danger.

"Listen closely, Trayhern. There's not much time. The captain, DEA and IOIC have decided Kit has to go underground. We don't have the manpower to provide her twenty-four-hour protection. She's going to have to disappear completely."

"Of course."

Cordeman's voice grew aggravated. "You still don't get it, do you? Kit's your responsibility now. I just talked with your commander, and we're all in agreement on the action to be taken."

"Fine, I'll go along with it. Just spell out the plan, Cordeman. Dante isn't going to waste any time getting to her."

"Tell me about it. Okay, here are your new orders. Kit is to go underground at your residence for the duration of Operation Storm. Since I haven't initiated the paperwork transferring Kit to the CG yet, that will be the ideal place for her to hide. It's been decided to issue fake orders transferring Kit up to Atlanta on special assignment. That will throw Dante off her trail. I'll be the only police contact with you and her. No one, other than me, the captain and your commander will know Kit's true whereabouts. Your residence will become a safe house for Kit. From there, she can ride with you to the ship and home again. It dovetails perfectly with the operation."

His fingers tightening around the phone, Noah whispered an epithet. How the hell could he keep a professional distance from Kit when she would be in his personal life? "There's no way you're putting her on my doorstep, Cordeman."

The supervisor laughed sharply. "Tell that to your commanding officer, Trayhern. Listen, this is coming down fast. You can't buck these orders. They've been approved all the way up the line. If I were you, I'd get over to Kit's home pronto, pack a few of her clothes and get her out of there before Dante shows up."

Kit heard the doorbell ring. She wiped her hands on a towel and placed it on the kitchen counter. It had to be Noah. Why had he sounded so grim on the phone earlier? Opening the door, she looked up at his hard features. He appeared harried—and aggravated.

"Come in," she invited. Her heart began a slow pound of dread as she read some undefinable emotion in his stormy eyes.

Taking off his officer's cap, Noah moved into the living room. Kit looked achingly beautiful in the raspberry-colored floor-length cotton gown she wore. Her hair was tousled, framing her oval face, her gray eyes large with concern. As she approached, he said, "I couldn't talk on the phone when I called you."

Kit tensed. "Something's wrong."

Obviously agitated, Noah ran his fingers across his chin. "Very wrong. Cordeman called me half an hour ago. Emilio Dante has been sprung from prison."

Gasping, Kit stared up at him in disbelief and confusion. Dante was free...and he had sworn to kill her the first chance he got! She shut her eyes tightly, trying to fight through the flood of fear. "My God..."

Noah saw her weave unsteadily. He reached out, gripping her arm. "Come on, sit down," he entreated huskily, leading her over to the couch. He sat down next to her.

"Dante's free. But how?" she cried.

Her fear became his. Until that moment, Noah hadn't realized just how much Kit had started to become someone important to him in an emotional sense. The feeling made him reel. Struggling to keep his voice calm and neutral, he told her what Cordeman had said.

"That means I have to disappear. I can't stay here...." Kit looked around the room. She'd spent little time in this house over the past five years, yet within one week she had grown to love its quiet beauty.

"I know. Cordeman and the DEA have already decided what's to be done," Noah began heavily.

"They want me to go to a motel under a fictitious name?"

"No. To my home. It will be your safe house for the duration of Storm."

"What?" Kit stared at him, her mouth dropping open. "You can't be serious!"

"I wish I wasn't," Noah confided, getting to his feet. "The DEA feels you'll be safe at my place. The paperwork transferring you to the CG was never processed. For once the slowness of bureaucracy is a blessing. Cordeman will issue fake orders sending you TAD to Atlanta. Besides, with you going out daily on the *Osprey* this will avoid a lot of transportation difficulties. You can ride to and from work with me." He saw the shock deepen in Kit's features.

Kit looked down at her hands. Her fingers were trembling. She might be physically safe at Noah's home, but her emotions were in danger. "But," she began in a strained voice, "can't you do something? Anything? I don't think us living together under one roof is such a good idea. We can't seem to spend an hour together without arguing."

"There's nothing either of us can do about it," he muttered. "Look, let's get you packed and out of here. There's no time to waste."

Rising, Kit turned to him. "This isn't going to work, dammit!"

All Noah's aggravation and frustration dissolved beneath the desperation in her gray eyes. Why the hell was he acting like this? He could see she was badly shaken by the news. Kit needed his maturity and protection right now, not his anger. "We'll make it work."

Her gaze followed every curve of his face. Despite the harsh set of his mouth, she found compassion in his eyes and heard it in his voice. Her heart said yes to the plan, but her wary mind screamed no. "Noah...this is going to be disastrous."

"I don't like it any more than you do."

Kit wanted to continue to protest, but she knew it was useless. Uncertain, she walked toward the bedroom. Too emotionally exhausted to argue further, she said, "Okay, but I'm not going to be your housekeeper and cook, Noah Trayhern."

He managed a curt nod. "You're a guest at my home. I'll treat you like one."

Kit swallowed against her constricted throat. "Give me a few minutes and I'll be ready to leave," she uttered tiredly.

"I feel ridiculous," Kit said to Noah as they drove toward his home.

He glanced over at her, struggling to sound optimistic. "As soon as you get over the initial shock, you'll be fine."

She had her doubts. The scenery along the freeway didn't impinge upon her inner turmoil, and Noah's closeness did nothing but emphasize her fragile emotions. She wasn't prepared for any kind of relationship with a man—professional or otherwise. Kit stole a quick glance at Noah's profile, lingering on his mouth. It turned up, and there were laugh lines at the corners of his eyes. The men she worked with didn't smile often.

"You know everything about me," she began awkwardly, "and I know nothing about you."

His sea-green eyes lightened. "I'll give you a hint—my friends refer to my home as 'Noah's ark.'"

Her brows drew down. "I'm in no shape for guessing games today. Mind explaining?"

"I'll let that be a surprise. What else do you want to know?"

Kit refused to yield to the implication in his husky voice. Further, she chose to ignore the word "home." She had always lived in a house, never a home. "Tell me about yourself," she insisted.

"Twenty-nine, single, black hair, green eyes—"

"Cut the stats. You sound like a sales pitch for some dating service."

"With my job responsibilities, I don't date much."

"Are you complaining?"

"Just a roundabout way of letting you know you won't be a third wheel at home."

Kit sank against the car seat, and as she closed her eyes, she suddenly felt very tired. "The more I get to know you, Noah, the less I understand about men," she admitted softly.

"You've worked with men all your life," Noah returned. *The dark side of them,* he thought. "Maybe I can show you a more positive side." He saw a slight upward curve of her lips. That was enough for him. Even in the bright afternoon sunlight that cascaded through the car window, Kit appeared drawn. "Go to sleep," he coaxed. "I'll wake you when we get home."

Kit released a sigh, the warmth of the sunlight making her drowsy. There was an incredible sense of protection surrounding her and she knew it was due to

Noah's presence. Even with Dante free, she knew she was safe with Noah. His words were like balm to her exhausted state and Kit quickly succumbed to sleep.

Noah glanced at Kit from time to time, keeping most of his attention on the traffic. In sleep she looked younger. It was hard to imagine that she was close to his own age; she looked twenty-four. Maybe that was why she had an ulcer: instead of allowing the tension of her job to show, she turned it inward on herself, like a dagger.

Groggily Kit forced her eyes open after a third gentle shake of her shoulder. Noah's male scent drifted into her sensitive nostrils and she inhaled it like a lost memory.

"Kit?" he called. "We're home."

Home...the word struck a responsive chord. If only she were really home...

"Come on, or I'll have to carry you in."

Viewing that as a threat, Kit forced herself to move, unbuckling the seat belt. She blinked, her lids heavy with sleep. "I feel as if I slept forever."

Noah opened the door to the Trans Am. "It was only about half an hour's worth."

She suppressed a yawn. "That long?"

"You needed it," he growled softly, climbing out of the sports car.

Kit was going to open her car door, but Noah got there first. "You don't have to do that," she protested, getting out.

He gave her a patient smile, cupping her elbow as he guided her up the walk.

Kit ignored the trace of irony she saw in Noah's face, looking instead at the house he called a home. It was a single-story brick bungalow with well-manicured hedges and several palms gracing the yard. Towering hibiscus bushes surrounded the house itself, their profusion of multicolored flowers creating a look of Eden.

Kit cast a glance up at him. "You do all the yard work alone?"

"Will wonders never cease?" Noah drawled, opening the latch on the gate and allowing her to enter the front yard.

"That tells me something about you."

Noah frowned. "What?"

"You may spend a lot of time at sea, but you also like putting your hands in the earth, as well."

"I like putting my hands on any living thing," he remarked cryptically as he fished the house key out of his pocket.

"That sounds threatening," Kit muttered.

"Relax. Okay, brace yourself," he warned, pushing the door open.

Kit frowned and began to ask why, when a barrage of brown, black and gray furry bodies assaulted her. The joyous bark of a dog and the meowing of two cats blended into a cacophony of greetings. Kit's eyes widened enormously as she was swamped by the cats running madly in circles between her legs. She heard

Noah laugh and he gripped her arm, guiding her skillfully through the animals.

The dog barked, leaping midair before them in the red tile foyer, and Kit realized with amazement that he had only three legs. A flood of compassion surged through her. Noah reached out, speaking in an authoritative, but nonetheless gentle tone. Immediately the black Doberman ceased his antics and calmly positioned himself in front of them, panting happily.

Kit looked up at Noah. "What is this? A zoo?"

He grinned, taking off his officer's cap and tossing it on the small mahogany desk nearby. "Noah's ark, remember?" He gestured toward the dog and two cats. "Meet my extended family. The dog's name is Tripoli. He's the general boss of my home when I'm not here and he's an outstanding watchdog."

Kit barely heard Noah's explanation, a pained expression on her face. "But look at him, Noah. He's got only three legs! My God, that's horrible...the poor thing."

Noah reached over to caress Kit's cheek, then chastised himself at the instinctive gesture. Kit invited intimacy. Disgruntled, he growled, "Let's look at the positives, shall we? No negatives. So his right front leg is missing. Tripoli gets around fine without it."

"But he's crippled!" Kit protested, a catch in her voice.

"He doesn't know that," Noah returned, catching her startled expression. "If you make him a cripple, he'll become one for you, Kit." He patted Tripoli affectionately, scratching a favorite place behind the dog's ear. Then Noah gave her a serious look. "But if you treat him as a whole dog, he'll be whole for you and won't know the difference."

Noah's philosophy rattled Kit. There was truth to his quietly spoken observation. She turned her attention to the cats, who milled about her feet, meowing out their own kind of welcome, begging for her attention. "It's a good thing I love animals," she groused, crouching in the hall to pet all of them.

Noah knelt beside her, acutely aware of the tenderness in her expression. "I knew you would."

"Did you, indeed?" Kit replied, hiding behind sarcasm.

This just wasn't going to work. She was snapping and defensive over his every comment. He picked up the first cat. "You hear that, Calico? This beautiful lady thinks I'm pulling her leg. What do you think?"

Calico promptly released a mournful meow as if on cue. Kit couldn't help but laugh as she reached over and petted the animal. She heard the cat wheezing heavily with each breath.

"Something's wrong with her...."

Noah nodded, placing Calico in her arms. "She came crawling up on my back porch last year during a hurricane. The vet diagnosed distemper. I thought she was going to die from it."

"And you pulled her through."

"Actually," Noah admitted, "Calico pulled herself through. She's got a good heart, and if you don't watch this little lady, she'll snuggle up beside you on the pillow at night. Callie prefers the softer things life has to offer."

Kit laughed helplessly, placing Calico on the highly polished red tile floor. Her heart softened as she stood watching Noah with his animals. Anyone who had this kind of devoted following couldn't be all bad. Animals were said to be living mirrors of their owner's temperament. "I wouldn't mind a furry body sharing my bed."

Noah's brow arched inquiringly.

Flushing, Kit stood nervously beneath his gaze. She could almost hear his rejoinder about him joining her in bed. The thought was startlingly heated. With every new discovery about Noah, her defenses melted just a little more, leaving her vulnerable to his appealing nature.

Picking up the second cat, Noah grinned. "This dainty little morsel is Tuna Boat." He placed her in Kit's waiting arms.

"She weighs a ton!" Kit exclaimed, hefting the twenty-pound long-haired gray cat.

"Yes, well, Tunie has never missed a meal in her life, as you can tell."

Kit tried not to be swayed by Noah and petted the worshipful cat. She studied the cat's face. "Oh, Noah . . ." she whispered, distraught. "Don't tell me she's—"

"Blind," Noah finished. "Some teenage boys were chasing her with sticks and struck her in the head down by the dock one morning before I went aboard the *Osprey*. I happened to see it, but by the time I got over there, the damage had been done. I took her to the vet and he said she was lucky to have survived the blow at all.'' He stroked the cat's head fondly as she nestled contentedly in Kit's arms. "She'll be blind the rest of her life."

Kit's gray eyes glittered with unexpected tears. "How can people pick on poor, defenseless animals that have no way to protect themselves?"

She was emotionally unpredictable. One more minus to their unworkable situation, Noah told himself. But Kit's unexpected compassion touched him deeply. "Tunie has the run of the front yard and back. She's in seventh heaven—she owns me, chows down twice a day and has a home."

"But she's blind!"

"Tunie doesn't know that. Put her down, Kit, and watch her navigate for a moment. This cat has memorized the entire layout of the house and yard." Noah shook his head, mystified. "I swear Tunie has all-terrain avionics inside that head of hers. She never runs into a tree or bush." He ruffled the cat's fur affectionately. "She's quite a little lady."

Kit rested her fingers against her throat, swallowing hard.

He gave her an intense look. "Animals touch you, don't they?"

She glared at him, then fixed her gaze on the cat. "Of course! Why should you be so surprised?"

"Now calm down. That wasn't meant as an accusation."

"It sounded like one."

"It was an obtuse compliment. Truce?"

Kit gave him a disgruntled look as she tore her eyes from Tunie. "All right," she relented. "Truce." Her voice lowered with feeling. "I don't believe all this. They're all disabled." And her eyes darkened upon him. "Am I one more cripple coming to your house, Noah?"

The tenor of her voice caught him off guard. His green gaze softened as he held her wavering stare. "In my eyes, no one here is crippled. Does that answer your question?"

Kit gulped down a lump, holding Tunie tightly. For some unknown reason, she identified strongly with the loving cat. "I feel like Tunie here," she admitted rawly. "Only my blindness to the narc business has left me spinning."

Noah nodded, understanding far more about her condition than he could let on. "You're surrounded by courage. Each one of these animals has pulled itself back to life with its own inner strength." He gave her an unsure look. Kit was too mercurial for his tastes. "Listen, let's get you settled. I've got some business to attend to back at the office. When I get home around seven, I'll make dinner. Deal?"

How could she say no? Kit wondered numbly, looking down at Tunie happily snuggled within her arms. Noah brought in her luggage and placed it in the brightly colored guest room that would be hers. Sunlight filtered through the pale green curtains. The bedspread was patterned with white daisies, yellow marigolds and rust-colored asters. The furniture was crafted from cherry wood, which added to the overall sense of richness of the decor. Kit stared at Noah's broad back as he placed the suitcases on the bed for her. Those shoulders could conceivably carry the weight of the world, she thought. Her heart blossomed with hope—a feeling she thought had been taken from her forever. Looking down, she realized the animals had crowded around her feet once more. She managed a laugh.

"Looks like I'm going to have all the help I need to unpack."

Her laughter was lilting, stealing through the barriers Noah had tried to erect. He straightened, forcing a smile. "Just watch Tunie. She has a terrible habit of plopping down in opened suitcases, open bureau drawers or on clothing that isn't hung up." Noah grimaced. "And I can't tell you how many times I've picked gray cat hairs off my uniform."

"Typical man—you throw your clothes anywhere it suits you."

Smarting under her observation, Noah halted at the entrance. "Get used to your new home while I'm gone," he muttered. "With all these characters here, I keep it clean or else. The bathroom is over there," he said, pointing toward a closed door.

"And your room?" Kit asked. The words were out before she could take them back.

Noah acted as if there were nothing wrong with her question. "On the other side of your bathroom." He gazed down at the animals, then up at her. "Take your time unpacking, get the layout of the house. Then I suggest a hot bath and some rest. You're still pale."

Kit wrinkled her nose. "I don't like being mothered, Noah."

His green eyes glinted with devilry. "Oh, yes, you do. You just don't know it. I'll see you later."

He was so sure of himself, and in her present state that unsettled her. "I'll see you at seven."

The lack of enthusiasm, even friendliness in her tone, left him uncomfortable. "Yeah. Seven." And he turned, leaving her bedroom.

After Noah left, Kit chastised herself. Her voice had sounded clipped and hard. Noah Trayhern was making her emotions fluctuate like a roller coaster. As she put away her jeans and tank tops and hung up what few dresses and skirts she owned, Kit attempted to sort out the past week.

Noah was a catalyst, she decided, for everything he came in contact with, judging from the animals sitting expectantly around the bed, watching her with aplomb. And whether Kit wanted to admit it or not, she felt protected with Noah's animal family. Taking a deep breath, she walked over to the bed, giving each cat a quick pat before wandering through the house. *Home,* she corrected herself. *Noah calls it a home.* It was going to be a battleground with them forced to live in such close quarters.

Kit mulled over that thought as she ambled down the hall. The feeling in his house made her admit it really was a home. She looked over her shoulder: Tuna Boat waddled in the lead, with Calico and Tripoli bringing up the rear. A tender smile pulled at her lips as she watched them follow her like a gaggle of loyal geese. Noah was right: they didn't recognize they were crippled, blind or shortchanged. Was love the ingredient that made them feel whole again?

Deep in thought, Kit wandered into Noah's bedroom by accident. Tuna Boat came and rested her plump fanny on Kit's foot. Calico wheezed on by, leaping up on the multicolored afghan spread across the large bed. Noah was like a prism, Kit decided as her gaze ranged around the room. Sunlight, when refracted through a crystal, revealed all the colors seen by the human eye. This room, this house, did not mirror the dark side of masculinity. Instead, like a prism, it showed light, color and sensitivity.

Several luxuriant Boston ferns hung from the ceiling, and potted plants graced the finely crafted cherrywood dresser. The warmth of the highly waxed mahogany floors only enhanced the feeling of life that made Kit want to stay in his room. A flood of guilt surged through her: she felt as if she were trespassing. Yet it was as if he had invited her to explore this personal side to himself. He trusted her!

By the time she had completed her exploration of the house, Kit was tired. Glancing at her watch, she saw it was almost three o'clock. Noah's suggestion of a hot bath sounded heavenly. At the door to the bathroom, Kit turned to the two cats tagging along with her.

"No," she told them firmly. "You are not following me in here."

As Kit shut the bathroom door and slid out of her clothes, her mind drifted back to Noah. She realized as she stepped into the hot, fragrant water that she had been on the receiving end of his hard, efficient side. This new and unexpected aspect involving his love of animals that had suffered beckoned to her. Noah was healing, whether she wanted to admit it or not. But could she keep her personal feelings for him at bay and maintain the decorum demanded of both of them in this unusual circumstance?

Getting out of the bath, Kit slipped into a silky lavender nightgown. Drowsy and feeling relaxed, she padded to the bed and lay down. As she tucked her hands beneath the pillow and closed her eyes, her last thoughts were of Noah and the miraculous effect he had upon her.

The sun was hot, making the humidity seem even higher than usual. Noah brushed a light film of sweat off his brow as he eased himself out of the Trans Am. He saw Tripoli at the picture window of his house as he sauntered up the walk. Glancing at his watch, he realized he was half an hour late. Kit was probably furious. Starving women made poor companions. Unlocking the front door, he was greeted by the Doberman. Noah leaned over to pet him, then took off his officer's cap and dropped it on the small desk.

"Where's Kit?" he asked. The dog leaped away, his claws clacking noisily on the wooden floor as he raced to the end of the hall toward the bedrooms. Noah followed him, steeling himself against Kit's anger at his lateness.

To his surprise, Kit didn't come out to meet him. He halted at the entrance to her bedroom, allowing his eyes to adjust to the gloom. The venetian blinds behind the green curtains had been pulled shut, and Noah felt his features relax. Kit lay asleep, a light quilt drawn up to her waist. Both cats were napping beside her.

Quietly entering the room, Noah stood over Kit and watched her sleep. He shouldn't be standing here; he ought to pretend she wasn't even in the house. But that was impossible, he admitted harshly to himself. While at dockside with the *Osprey* crew, he'd thought constantly of Kit being here in his home. Oddly, just getting to see her helped evaporate the confusion of his feelings. He narrowed his eyes with concern. Even in the semidarkness her skin was pale, drawn tightly across her cheekbones. The shadows beneath her eyes were still in evidence, and Noah tried to curb his worry. Her lips were parted, stress no longer drawing in the corners. *So,* he thought, *you really do want to laugh.* She looked like a lost, helpless waif on the huge expanse of the bed. Noah leaned over and pulled the quilt up around her shoulders, tucking it in so that she would remain warm despite the coolness of the central air-conditioning.

Straightening, Noah ordered himself to leave. He had to before he reached out to caress her cheek. Every time he got around Kit, he seemed to go into a tailspin. She must have taken a bath—her hair was slightly curled, easing the angular planes of her face and creating a softer look to her features. The powerful need to will away the pain she still carried caught him off balance.

He didn't want to leave Kit's room, but he made himself move. How Kit, as a woman, had survived five years in the narc trench warfare was beyond him. He kept the door to her bedroom open so that the animals could come and go as they pleased. As he walked down the hall to his own room, Noah admitted that Kit affected him deeply. No woman had ever reached out and unraveled him like this. Somehow, he was going to have to hide all those feelings from her. But how?

Kit felt the warm roughness of a man's hand moving across her shoulder. Drowsily she forced open her eyes. Even in the darkness she was aware of the intensity of Noah's gaze as he leaned over her.

"I thought I'd better get you up for a bite to eat," he explained in a low voice. "Then you can go back to bed."

She fought the drugged feeling of tiredness, slowly becoming aware of his presence. A fresh ribbon of emotion squeezed from her heart as she silently stared up at him. Noah gave her stability, and something more. "Wh-what time is it?"

"Almost 9:00 p.m."

"Nine?" Her eyes widened and she struggled into a sitting position. It dawned on her that she was wearing a revealing gown with a low-cut neck, and heat rushed into her cheeks. What was he doing in *her* bedroom? And then, with a pang, Kit realized she hadn't shut the door, so how could he knock and announce his presence? She pulled her knees upward. Sudden shyness gripped her when she saw the undisguised hunger in his eyes.

Noah placed himself in check. Gone were all of Kit's defenses. She sat shyly before him like a child-woman just awakening from a wonderful dream. Grimly he forced himself to step away from the bed.

"I wanted you to get something to eat before we tucked you in for a good night's sleep," he told her, his voice gruff.

"'We'?" Kit asked, her voice husky.

Noah gestured to the foot of the bed. "The cats slept with you."

Kit laughed. It was a clear, uninhibited laugh, straight from her heart. And the rich sound coming from her filled her with an inexplicable joy. Her eyes crinkled as she met Noah's green gaze. "I don't believe this, Noah. I feel as if I'm in some kind of dream. Your animals are like little guardians." Her smile died on her lips as she searched his shadowed face.

"You're coming out of a five-year tunnel of darkness."

"I'm just beginning to realize how badly I buried myself in my work. You're right. It was a horrible tunnel."

"Life doesn't have to be a dark, moody scene, Kit. There can be light and laughter in this crazy-quilt world of ours." He managed a smile. "There can be light even in the worst sort of darkness."

Kit shut her eyes and turned her head away. "At first I thought you were just like Pete."

Noah shoved his hands into the pockets of his jeans. "Oh?" What she thought of him meant more than he cared to admit.

Kit rested her cheek against her drawn-up knees and stared blankly at the wall. "You're driven just as he was. And you have something to prove because of your family tragedy. Pete was always striving to prove he was better than anyone else. His work was his entire life." Releasing a broken sigh, Kit raised her head and gazed up at Noah. "Maybe I'm wrong about you to a degree. This house is lived in and cared for. All the plants are healthy and trimmed. I noticed you had a bunch of seedlings on the windowsill in the kitchen.... Your officer image doesn't fit the Noah Trayhern who lives in this house."

Relieve to hear she didn't think he was another Pete Collins, Noah grinned. "Don't take my officer image too lightly. Remember, I come from a family with a two-hundred-year tradition of military service."

Although hungry for information about him, Kit quelled her curiosity. Even in the shadows, Noah had a kind face when he allowed that officer's mask to slip. The man who stood relaxed in front of her was her boss. Kit couldn't still the suffused happiness that surfaced unexpectedly within her. "Let me put my robe on, and I'll join you in a few minutes," she promised.

Chapter Five

Kit shuffled into the kitchen. Hands thrust deeply into the blue velour pockets of her robe, she stood uncertainly at the entrance. Noah had just placed a seafood salad at the table, and he motioned for her to come and sit down.

He saw a smile light her eyes, erasing the tension around her mouth. "Come on in," he invited.

"Somehow," Kit commented, sitting down and picking up the royal blue linen napkin, "I think I've got the better end of our deal. This is more than a safe house. This salad looks pretty good."

Pouring her some coffee, Noah sat down opposite her. Funny, how Kit made the house feel warm and comfortable with her quiet presence. "My mother made all three of us kids learn how to cook," he noted wryly.

Smiling, Kit picked up the fork. Suddenly she was famished. The combination of crab, lobster and shrimp on a bed of fresh lettuce was incredibly appealing. "Good for her."

"Did yours?"

She grinned and scooped a forkful of crab into her mouth. There was amusement in Noah's thoughtful green eyes. The rapport he established with her was molten, heating the inner fires of her heart. "Yes, me and my older brothers."

"Good for her," he repeated.

"I'll help around here with house duties, Noah. I don't intend to be a bad house guest."

"This house is just like a ship. Every crew member has responsibilities. We'll set up a system and share the chores. You're not the type to escape duty, anyway," he mused, sipping his coffee.

"You're right. Noah, this is really disconcerting."

"What is?"

Kit jabbed her fork into a piece of lobster. "You have an entire personnel file on me. I have absolutely nothing on you."

"I'm an open book."

Kit gave him a dark look. "Sure you are."

He sat back, the silence pleasant despite her growling. "I figure with the time we're going to have to spend with each other, you'll probably find out more about me than you'd like to know."

Kit wasn't so sure. "To tell you the truth, I'm feeling bad about cluttering up your personal life by using your place as a safe house."

Noah toyed with his cup, turning it slowly around. "I don't have much of a personal life, except that I visit my parents in Clearwater once a month, or open up one of the guest rooms to my sister, Alyssa."

Kit finished the salad and pushed the plate aside, then picked up her coffee cup. "It sounds like you're close to your family, the way I am to mine."

He snorted softly. "Believe me, if we hadn't been close in these five years since Morgan disappeared, I don't know how any of us would have survived."

She nodded sympathetically, recalling the press about Morgan Trayhern's defection to North Vietnam. Every time the topic came up, Noah's eyes reflected grief and sadness. Kit hurt for him.

"My father just retired from the Minneapolis Police Department," she offered, not wanting to dig into something so sensitive. "I have three brothers who are in the highway patrol."

"Family tradition runs strong in you, too."

"Don't sound so unhappy about it. They like what they're doing."

He shrugged, wanting, unsuccessfully, to keep their talk impersonal. "I wasn't thinking about them. Take a look at you— I think family pressure pushed you into a career you really weren't cut out for."

Kit studied him for a long time before answering. Noah had made the comment with feeling, not hurled it as an accusation. "Lately I've been thinking about that possibility," she admitted quietly. "What about you? Are you happy in your chosen career?"

"Yes. I put in long hours to keep my record spotless. You get ahead in the Coast Guard by making yourself outstanding in some way. I've had to work extra hard because of what happened to Morgan."

"You work at your job twenty-four hours a day, leaving no time for a personal life."

"You've done the same thing," he parried.

Kit got up and went to the drain board, leaning against it, coffee cup in hand. "Maybe we're both like Pete Collins and don't want to admit it."

"Maybe you project Collins on every man you meet."

"Touché. Maybe I do."

Disgruntled, Noah rose and arranged the dirty dishes in the dishwasher. Why did he get nettled when she compared him to Collins? He was nothing like him!

"What's on the agenda for tomorrow?" Kit asked, realizing he was upset.

"It's the weekend," he snapped.

"I didn't know it made any difference to you." Kit saw the anger flash momentarily in his eyes and knew she'd blundered into sensitive territory. Wearily she said, "I guess it does."

"I try to work five days a week, Kit, not seven. But I've had to prove myself. Other times we're at sea for an extended period." Noah felt some of the anger drain away as he noticed Kit struggling to smooth over the tension between them.

"So what do you usually do on weekends?" Kit knew that since she was in hiding, she would have to remain solely at the house or on the *Osprey*.

"If I haven't taken on any extra projects at headquarters, I work with wood and make furniture, or take my boat out to a cove and snorkel for dinner. What do you do?"

She shrugged and set the cup on the drain board. "Lately I've watched too much television. This is the first time I've had a series of weekends off in years. I guess I'll find out, won't I?"

The sudden unhappiness in her eyes bothered him. He rested his hands on his hips, studying her. "I was going to plant those seedlings tomorrow along the front of the house."

"I like the idea of you planting flowers. Need some help?"

There was life in her eyes, and Noah found himself drowning in their soft dove-gray color. Jerking himself back from his spiraling attraction to Kit, he muttered, "If you want to help, you can."

"I'd love to. It's been a long time since I've dug my fingers into the earth, or even sat in the sunshine doing something like that."

He heard the enthusiasm in her tone and was unable to stop a smile from curving the corners of his mouth. "Get some sleep, Kit. I'll see you in the morning."

* * *

Cordeman's call at eight in the morning rousted Noah out of sleep. He turned over, groping for the phone.

"Trayhern," he muttered.

"This is Cordeman. I'm calling from a pay phone because I don't want our conversation tapped by the wrong parties."

Noah sat up, instantly alert. The sheet fell away, exposing his naked chest. "What is it?" He wiped the sleep from his eyes, his heart taking on an urgent beat.

"Nothing's wrong, Lieutenant. I'm just calling to make sure your house guest arrived safely."

Eyeing the clock on the dresser, Noah bit back a curse. "She's fine," he ground out.

"Good, because word is Dante's out lookin' for Kit. Another one of our snitches brought us the news late last night. I don't want her to show her face in Miami. You understand, Trayhern? She's not to make phone calls, or answer your phone, either."

Pushing strands of hair off his brow, Noah dangled his legs over the edge of the bed. Sunlight streamed through the windows. "Look, Cordeman, I know standard operating procedure on this, so don't lecture me like I was some rookie cop."

"I just want to make damn sure she's safe. The only place she goes is to and from the dock."

"I've got a boat at a marina outside Miami. Some weekend I plan to take her out on it for the day. Any problem with that?"

"Just keep her low profile, Trayhern. I have a DEA agent who is in position to retrieve info on Garcia—if he's able to get it back to us. Operation Storm is officially initiated as of now. That three weeks you wanted for her is out of the question with Dante loose.''

"Dammit." Noah rubbed the growth of beard on his face savagely. Cordeman was right. Dante would renew activity with Garcia now that he was out on bail. "I'm planning to get her on board the *Osprey* Monday."

"Fine. She's got this weekend to rest up then."

Noah wanted to say that Kit needed a hell of a lot more than that, but it was useless. "Anything else?"

"Yeah, one more thing."

"What?"

"Keep all this stuff about Dante from Kit. She saw the bastard blow Pete away."

"Don't worry, I intend to try to allow her a place to heal, Cordeman."

The supervisor chuckled. "Yeah, the word's out on you, Trayhern—you're a real in-fighter for your people. I oughta know."

Grimly Noah said, "I still want you to do everything in your power to make the next three weeks as easy as possible on Kit. She's fragile...."

"I'll do my best. You two have a good weekend. I've got a feeling Kit needs a Sir Lancelot right now."

Sir Lancelot. Noah dropped the phone back into the cradle, his mood black. Grumbling, he got up, took a hot shower, shaved and then dressed in a pair of old, faded jeans and a red polo shirt.

Opening the door, he waited for the rush of animals that always came. No one was in sight. The entire house was still. Frowning, he wondered where everyone was. Usually the cats were meowing at his bedroom door, with Tripoli nearby. Padding down the hall in his bare feet, Noah saw that Kit's bedroom door was ajar. The scent of coffee wafted on the air, and he inhaled the delicious aroma.

Moving to the kitchen, he saw that coffee had just been put on to brew. Kit must be up. Glancing out the back door, he frowned and drew to a halt. There in the yard was Kit, playing Frisbee with Tripoli. The two cats sat on the sidelines like little spectators. Dressed in a pink tank top and jeans, she was laughing as the Doberman raced after her, chasing her merrily around the huge yard, trying to grab the Frisbee out of her hand.

Noah's eyes narrowed as he watched Kit play tag with the frolicking dog. Her cheeks were flushed, her eyes alive with joy, and her laughter was like music to his ears. He poured two cups of coffee and edged open the door, standing at the screen. Tripoli lunged at the Frisbee in Kit's right hand, trying to tug it free. Startled by the dog's unexpected move, Kit tripped over her own feet and fell.

She hit the dew-soaked lawn with a thud, rolling to take any shock from the fall. Laughing as Tripoli raced around her, Frisbee in his mouth, Kit tried to snatch it back from the dog. Tears ran down her cheeks at Tripoli's endearing antics. Finally he came and lay at her side, dropping the toy nearby. Panting happily, Tripoli licked her hand.

"Oh, boy," Kit gasped, sitting up and running her fingers through her unruly hair, "you are one tough dog, Tripoli." She reached out, throwing her arms around his neck, pressing her cheek against the dog's head. "What a love you are... I never realized how much I missed animals until just now...."

Kit pulled deep drafts of air into her lungs. She wasn't used to fifteen minutes of running and jumping like this. But Tripoli had brought the Frisbee to her while she was making the coffee, and she hadn't been able to resist his silent plea. She closed her eyes, running her hands down his sleek black back, thanking him silently for his companionship.

Noah moved out into the yard, stopping just short of where Kit and Tripoli sat on the grass together. He was suddenly envious of the Doberman as he watched her stroke the dog with such obvious affection. "If I'd known you liked exercise, I'd have made plans to take you jogging with me."

Kit's head jerked up and her widened eyes settled on Noah. She shivered, wildly aware of that green flame of hunger in his gaze once again. Tripoli left her arms, going to his master's side. "Noah..." she began lamely. Again she felt as if she were invading his private life.

He crouched in front of her, handing her a cup of steaming coffee. Did Kit know how pretty she was? She looked like a young girl right now, her hair tousled and eyes shining with happiness. "Do you always get up this early on a Saturday morning?" he demanded, sipping his coffee.

"Thanks," she whispered, taking the cup. Lowering her lashes, she was unable to meet his disapproving gaze. "Uh...well, I usually sleep all day." A nightmare about Emilio Dante had awakened her at six, but she didn't want to tell Noah that. She forced herself to look up. Noah made her feel good about herself as a woman. No, he made her vibrantly aware that she *was* a woman. "It was just such a beautiful morning that I couldn't resist Tripoli's invitation to play Frisbee." She grinned. "As you can see, he won."

"He's a keen player."

"Like his owner, no doubt."

Noah nodded, enjoying the intimacy that had sprung up between them. "I play for keeps," he said amicably. His gaze dropped to Kit's parted lips, and he wondered for the hundredth time what it would be like to kiss her. She was so damned provocative and appealing, sitting there in the yard with bits of grass entangled in the ebony strands of her hair. Against his better judgment, he leaned forward and began to pick the green bits from her curls.

Stunned by Noah's gesture, Kit inhaled sharply. He was utterly male, his jeans hugging his lower body, effectively outlining his well-developed thighs. The polo shirt revealed just how powerful his chest really was. His arms were tightly muscled and covered with dark hair. Noah was built like a boxer: lean, tight and well proportioned, standing at least six-two. There was nothing to dislike about him physically, she decided lamely.

"It's nice to see an adult who can play like a child," he teased, plucking the last of the grass from her hair.

Shaken by his nearness, Kit said, "When you've got three brothers, you learn to tumble with them, not play with dolls and stay clean."

"A beautiful woman in tomboy's clothes."

Kit had never thought of herself as beautiful—until now. "I guess growing up with brothers brought out the tomboy in me," she murmured, getting to her feet. Noah was too close, too male for her ever since he had touched her hair. She had to keep her distance.

Disappointed that Kit had scrambled to her feet, Noah rose and straightened. He saw her sudden nervousness and decided that she was right: this was a business arrangement, not a friendship or love relationship. "You make a good cup of coffee," he said, trying to get on neutral ground with her once again.

Kit brushed off the seat of her pants. "Coffee's something I can't live without."

"Makes two of us." Noah smiled down at her. "Hungry? I make a pretty mean breakfast of whole grain pancakes with maple syrup."

Groaning, Kit fell into step with Noah. "Don't tell me you're one of those health nuts!"

"Afraid so."

"I'm a junk food addict."

He caught her rueful smile, thinking how sweet her lips looked when they curved upward. "Opposites attract, they say."

Kit wasn't sure what he meant by that enigmatic statement. "Opposites or not, I'm starved."

Her enthusiasm was infectious. Noah couldn't recall feeling this elated. Even his step felt lighter. "Well, you'd better eat plenty, because I'm going to put you to work in the flower garden after breakfast," he threatened good-naturedly.

Noah chastised himself; he was getting friendly with her again. But how could he help it? There was a refreshing quality to Kit. She simply invited a man to lower his walls and be himself with her.

"I can help you with breakfast," Kit offered once they were in the kitchen.

"No, that's all right. Just sit down and relax."

Her mouth quirked. "Noah, I don't expect to be waited on hand and foot."

Busying himself gathering the ingredients, he nodded. "Fair enough. You can clean up the dishes afterward and put them in the dishwasher."

The warmth they had shared dissolved as they fell back into their assigned roles. Dejectedly Kit sat down at the table. One minute Noah was like the warmth of sunshine around her, the next he was grumpy and defensive. Why was he shifting from one extreme to the other? Frowning, she asked, "Are you *sure* I'm not a royal pain in the rear for invading your personal space?"

Pouring milk into the pancake mixture, Noah stirred the contents in a bowl. "Positive."

His guard was up and well in place again. Kit sighed. "Don't you have a girlfriend who comes over here every once in a while?"

"No girlfriend. The kind of life I lead doesn't encourage many long-term relationships. Most women don't like their men at sea three to seven days at a time."

Kit found that hard to believe, but didn't say so. Besides, she felt an unexpected monumental relief at his admittance. Rubbing her eyes, she sank into silence. She didn't have the strength to overcome Noah's sudden retreat from her.

After breakfast, which took place in stilted silence, Kit said, "I need to talk to Chuck Cordeman. I know the routine about not using the phone, but I've got to talk to him."

Scowling, Noah got up and poured himself another cup of coffee. "Why do you need to speak to him?"

Girding herself, Kit met his troubled gaze when he came back to the table and sat down. "Look, Noah...this isn't going to work."

"What isn't?"

"This," she said, gesturing around the kitchen. "You and me under one roof together. Ever since I got here, I've felt this tension around you. I feel trapped. I feel odd about doing anything for fear you'll disapprove. Like this morning, when I was playing with Tripoli. I felt as if I were somehow trespassing." She shrugged, gripping the mug in her hands. "You're one of those men with his life in a certain order, and you don't like someone coming in and messing up the continuity. I understand that. I even agree." Kit gave him a pleading look, noticing the turmoil in his eyes. "Let me go to some motel nearby and stay there. I can handle it. This isn't the first time I've had to do a safe house routine."

Getting a grip on his emotions, Noah held her gaze. "Look," he began in a low voice, "I don't mean to make you feel you have to be a shadow here." Noah couldn't tell her the real reason for his abruptness: if he didn't put that wall between them, he would pull her into his arms. A white lie was better than the truth in this case, he decided. Kit didn't need any more pressure on her, and yet, he realized, he was unintentionally applying it to her. "I'll admit that having someone here is different, but I'll adjust, Kit. Just ride this out with me, okay? I'll get used to you being underfoot." He snorted. "Besides, there's no way you're staying in a dingy motel room like a trapped animal in a cage."

Searching his face hard, Kit sensed his ambivalence. Her voice came out soft. "I don't want to intrude on your life, Noah. Neither of us expected to be thrown together like this. I—I just don't know how to act around you."

Picking up her hand, Noah squeezed it. "Listen to me, Kit. You do what feels right for you. I promised Cordeman a place for you to heal, and I mean it."

Just his touch sent unexpected tears to her eyes. She hastily lowered her gaze so he couldn't see them and pulled her hand out of his, poignantly aware of the warmth and strength of it. "Are you sure?"

"Yeah, I'm sure," Noah said, getting to his feet. "Don't take my change of moods personally, Kit. Right now, my sister, Alyssa, is under a lot of pressure at Pensacola. She's got a flight instructor who's trying to wash her out of the program. I'm worried for her."

It was on the tip of her tongue to whisper that Noah cared a great deal about the people in his life. Looking up, Kit managed a wan smile. "If Alyssa's anything like you, I know she'll hang in there."

Relief washed through Noah. He and Kit had just surmounted a small crisis. Somehow he had to wall off his moodiness from her so she could relax and heal. "Aly's going to be coming down here one of these weekends soon. I'm sure you'll get to meet her." He managed a genuine smile. "In fact, she's a lot like you."

"How do you see me?" Kit asked, getting up to attend to her portion of the kitchen chores.

"Loyal, hardworking and overresponsible."

"And Alyssa's like that?" She picked up the plates from the table.

Chuckling, Noah nodded. "Very much so. I think you two will have a lot in common." Wanting to add that Kit had that same kind of vulnerability Aly possessed, Noah decided to remain silent. However, Kit didn't have Aly's bulldog attitude, he reminded himself. Their tenacity was a Trayhern hallmark. Kit had run out of emotional stamina and strength after four years with Pete Collins. There was nowhere else for her to pull that extra strength from in order to survive, as Aly had done in the past. As all Trayherns had done at some point in their lives, he admitted.

After she finished loading the dishwasher, he said, "Let's go plant those seedlings, shall we?"

Kit nodded, wiping her hands on a towel. Whatever had been bothering Noah was now gone. His face was open and expressive once again. "You don't know how much I've looked forward to this, Noah."

Noah's heart wrenched in his chest at her quietly spoken admittance. Once again the desire to reach out and take her in his arms was excruciating. But Kit needed a little attention, a little care right now. Instead he squeezed her shoulder momentarily and then said, "Come on, let's find out if you've got a green thumb or not."

Chapter Six

It was Monday morning and time to go to work. Noah smiled to himself as Kit walked at his right shoulder down the long, concrete dock. At the end of it was the *Osprey*.

"Excited?" Noah asked. The morning sky was bathed in colors of pale peach and flaming orange.

Kit breathed in the salty air. "No, I'm worried about seasickness." The sun was up, creating a glare across the quiet channel waters where the Coast Guard station sat near the Atlantic Ocean.

"You've got that seasickness patch behind your ear?" Noah glanced down at her. Kit had worn her one-piece dark blue police uniform replete with revolver. He had relented and allowed her to wear the weapon. Sometimes orders could be bent. And because she was in uniform, the revolver seemed a natural addition. Nevertheless she looked feminine as hell, her unruly black hair emphasizing her dancing gray eyes. His mind wandered back over the weekend. There had been a truce of sorts. He had taken all the strain upon himself, making Kit feel she was an indispensable partner around his home. She had responded beautifully, and her laughter was all he'd needed as a reward.

"Yes, it's in place." Kit pressed the small bandage hidden behind her left ear, hoping it would stop any seasickness. She looked at the SES that sat like an elegant steed at the end of the dock. Painted a medium gray color, the *Osprey* was huge. Crewmen were already on board, moving around on the decks, performing the jobs that would ready the *Osprey* for a day at sea.

On the enclosed bridge of the vessel, Noah introduced Ensign Joe Edwards, his second-in-command, to Kit. The younger officer, who had just graduated from the academy, blushed deeply when he shook her hand. Joe was just as taken with Kit's quiet demeanor and natural beauty as he was, Noah decided. If Kit noticed Joe's blush, she didn't react to it as she took a seat not far from the helm.

"What's on the hot sheet today?" Noah asked, taking his place at the large steel helm. He always guided the *Osprey* out of dock and into the channel that led to the ocean.

Joe picked up the hot-sheet list. "The DEA has added two more vessels is all, Skipper." He smiled over at Kit, handing her the clipboard. "You might as well take a look at this, ma'am. They list names of boats or ships that have been known to carry marijuana bales. Sometimes we run into the vessels out at sea, and we order them to drop anchor so we can make a search."

Noah ordered his crew to cast off. The morning was clear and cloudless, and he found himself happy that Kit was with them. Under his hand the *Osprey* moved away from her berth. The hull of the ship sliced cleanly through the waters of the channel. Up ahead was the greenish-blue expanse of the Atlantic Ocean. Once clear of the channel, Noah would let Edwards take over and they'd head south, moving around the tip of the Florida peninsula to begin their hunt for boats carrying drugs.

Kit felt her stomach begin to roll the moment the *Osprey* moved out into the ocean. She swallowed hard, praying that her reaction was only temporary.

After Noah turned over the *Osprey* to Edwards, he walked over to her. "You're looking a little green," he noted, taking in Kit's once flushed features, which were now drawn with tension. He rested his hand on the back of the steel chair where she sat, aware how much easier he found it to deal with her professionally in the atmosphere of his boat and crew.

"It's nothing," Kit murmured, swallowing hard. She forced a smile. "How about giving me the grand tour of this lady?"

"Sure?" He looked intently into her trusting, soft gray eyes, and took a deep breath, controlling the surge of feelings she aroused in him.

Slipping off the seat, Kit nodded. "Very sure."

Both bulkhead doors to the bridge were open, allowing the warm, humid ocean air to circulate. Noah stepped out onto the deck. The *Osprey* was barely moving up and down; the ocean was glassy smooth. If Kit was seasick now, would she handle the moderate sea that usually came up every afternoon when the winds picked up?

Kit fought valiantly to ignore her roiling stomach as Noah led her around the deck. On the bow sat a fifty-caliber machine gun on a tripod, reminding her that the Coast Guard's mission could turn ugly. And then she looked down at the revolver she carried at her waist. She hadn't been in uniform since her graduation from the academy five years ago. It felt strange to be wearing the bulky black leather belt and holster around her waist. But it was necessary, she reminded herself. Still, the idea of a gun battle sickened her.

"Below deck we have crew quarters, a small galley and the weapons area," Noah said, gesturing for Kit to climb down the stairs. With each passing minute Kit looked worse, her face paler.

"This is quite a ship," Kit admitted once on the lower deck. The SES was immaculate. Noah Trayhern ran a tight vessel from what Kit could tell, and the men obviously respected him. He was a natural leader.

Taking her by the elbow, Noah led her down one passage. "The *Osprey* is the new generation cutter designed for drug work. Her hull is built to take the waves without a lot of yawing or rolling."

"I feel like everything's rolling."

"You're looking worse. Do you want to lie down for a while?"

Kit shook her head. "I'm sure it will pass, Noah." They arrived amidships, where several rows of bunks were built into the hull.

"These are the crew's quarters. They're cramped to say the least."

"Looks like a can of sardines if you ask me," Kit joked. The *Osprey* rolled beneath them and instinctively she placed her hand on her stomach.

The gesture wasn't lost on Noah. "Let's go to my cabin," he suggested, leading her past the crew's quarters. He pushed open a bulkhead door halfway down the narrow passageway, revealing a small room with a bed, a table and chair and a desk, all bolted to the floor. "Go on in."

Nausea stalked her and she didn't try to argue. He led her to the bunk and sat her down. "Rest awhile. When people get seasick they either want to stay up in the fresh air or lie down."

The bunk was inviting. Kit gave him a sheepish glance. "I think I'll lie down. I'm sorry, Noah."

He reached out, barely caressing her hair in a gesture meant to give her solace. Kit looked positively miserable. "Don't be. Just take it easy. I doubt if there will be any action today, but if we need you, I'll send one of the crew down to get you. Otherwise, rest."

Feeling as if she had disappointed him, Kit nodded. "Thanks." After he left, Kit unbuckled the cumbersome belt and holster, placing them on the desk. Lying down did help to a degree, but the fact that even the most modern drug wasn't going to help her was a big disappointment. She'd warned Noah she was strictly a landlubber.

"Where's Detective Anderson?" Joe asked when Noah reappeared on the bridge.

"Lying down in my cabin."

Nodding his sandy-haired head, Joe said, "She doesn't look very seaworthy, does she?"

Sitting down, Noah picked up the hot-sheet list. "No, she doesn't."

"Pretty, though."

"Very."

"For being from the police department, she's got a nice way about her," Edwards added, checking the compass and lightly turning the helm to keep the *Osprey* on course.

Kit was nice in many unexpected ways, Noah grudgingly admitted. "Especially for having been an undercover cop for five years."

Edwards whistled, his blue eyes crinkling with surprise. "Her? An undercover agent? You gotta be kidding, Skipper."

"I wish I was. She's not cut out for it."

"No kidding. Man, we've seen some hard agents, and Kit—I mean, Detective Anderson—just doesn't fit that bill of goods."

Smiling to himself, Noah returned to the paperwork at hand. He noticed Joe had slipped and called her Kit. She had the same mesmerizing effect on everyone, it seemed, himself included. The rows of radios surrounding them on the bridge were fairly quiet. They would get noisy if a drug boat were spotted.

"Don't let her fool you, though," Noah warned him. "She's survived five years in the trenches and is alive to tell about it."

"Yeah, but what's it done to her, Skipper? We both know the undercover world is hell on an agent."

And Kit had gone over the edge, Noah wanted to add, but he didn't. He had gotten permission to tell Edwards that his home was a safe house for Kit. But the rest of the crew would never know; as far as they were concerned, she was just another police officer interfacing with the Coast Guard. A well-kept secret would keep Kit safe. "Her health isn't what it should be," he said in answer to Joe's question. That wasn't a total lie, but it wasn't really the full truth, either. Noah felt himself becoming even more protective of Kit, wanting to shield her in every way possible.

"Well, she's quite a lady in my book. I'm kind of glad she's going to be with us during Operation Storm."

Placing the clipboard on the console, Noah watched his crewmen on deck for several moments before responding to Joe. "I don't know if she's going to be glad to be with us," he finally said ruefully.

Edwards chuckled. "Yeah, if she's seasick even taking that drug, she might get to hate this assignment real fast."

The brilliant blue-green depths of the ocean were darkening, telling Noah they were moving away from the coast. The waves were barely two feet in height; it was a perfect day. "I'll check on her around noon. Maybe she'll be feeling better by then," Noah said. He could send one of the crewmen to look in on Kit, but he wanted to do it himself. Glancing at his watch, he saw that it was 8:30 a.m.

In some respects, the day was going to drag because Kit wasn't there at his side. Musing on how much Kit had already made herself a part of his life, Noah shook his head. What kind of magic did she wield? He felt as if his life were spinning completely out of his control. Yet he had to maintain a professionalism or jeopardize his career. He had enemies who wanted to embarrass him because of Morgan. No, somehow he had to walk that razor-fine line, help Kit back on her feet and carry out his duties in the meantime. He glanced at his watch one more time, restless and wanting to make sure Kit was all right.

The bulkhead door opened, then closed. Kit stirred from sleep and drowsily opened her eyes. Noah stood nearby, his face etched with shadows.

"Uh..." Kit struggled into a sitting position. "I didn't mean to fall asleep."

Noah sat down on the lone chair in the room, studying her intently. Kit's eyes were still heavy with sleep, her mouth soft and inviting. The urge to reach out and brush the hair off her brow almost got the better of him. He kept his hands resting on his thighs. "When you get seasickness, sleep is the best thing. How are you feeling?"

Groggily Kit took stock of herself. "My stomach's more settled, thank God."

Smiling slightly, Noah nodded. "Good. It's noon and we're going to be dishing up chow pretty soon. Do you feel like joining us?"

She didn't, but Kit refused to allow her present condition to control her. "Sure. Just give me a minute to freshen up." She ran her fingers through her hair, trying to tame it back into place.

Rising, Noah opened the door. Kit still didn't look too good. The walls she usually kept erected were gone. Maybe she was finally trusting him enough to be herself. "I'll see you in the galley, then," he said, his voice strained.

The tension between them was broken. Kit watched him disappear out the door, shutting it quietly behind him. She hadn't slept at all the night before, with dreams of Emilio Dante plaguing her. As she stood up and pressed her hand against her stomach, she wondered if some of her reaction to the ocean was really fatigue in disguise. Ever since she had found out Dante was loose and hunting for her, she barely slept at night. Kit ran her fingers through her hair one more time.

The mirror image staring back at her wasn't that of the Kit she used to know. Even in the dark blue uniform replete with silver badge and name plate, Kit didn't feel very much like a police officer anymore. What was happening to her? Being around Noah was exposing all her soft and feminine emotions. She no longer felt strong and confident. Instead she had an urgent need for some gentleness and peace in her life. Noah gave her that. Touching her arched brow, Kit looked deeply into her shadowed eyes. The old Kit Anderson was dying. In her place was this new person, this new woman, who had a serenity the old Kit hadn't felt in five years.

Confused by the myriad changes within her, Kit turned around. She stared at the revolver in the holster. Her mind told her to put it on and wear it. The rest of her recoiled from the ugly-looking weapon that could take a life. Fingers trembling, Kit reached down and reluctantly strapped on the hardware. The belt and holster hung heavily around her waist like an anchor. Disturbed and not understanding why, Kit left the cabin, heading toward the galley.

Four *Osprey* crewmen sat at one of three tables, eagerly consuming their noontime meal. Noah sat alone, his full tray in front of him. Kit nodded to the crew and made her way across the steel deck.

Noah stood as she approached, noticing her shyness in front of his men. "Sit down, Kit. Freddy is our cook on board. He's made—"

"Please," Kit protested quietly, "I don't want any food, Noah." She gave him an apologetic look as she sat down opposite him. "I can't handle it right now."

"How about some fruit juice?" he suggested.

Her stomach was beginning to roll once more. Was sleep the only way to spare herself this misery? When she saw Noah's frown, she knew she'd have to eat or drink something in order to erase the worry she saw in his eyes. "I think I can get down some tomato juice."

Freddy, a red-haired, freckle-faced crewman, brought over a small glass with a slice of lemon for Kit. She thanked him and busied herself squeezing in the citrus juice. Noah began eating with relish. Swallowing hard, Kit cast about for some topic that would get her mind off her damnable stomach.

"Spotted any drug boats yet?"

"No, it's quiet so far."

The tomato juice was cold and tasted good. Kit sipped it slowly. "How do you intercept these smugglers?"

Noah smiled lightly. "Sheer luck, usually. No, that isn't always so. Sometimes a Navy P3 subhunter airplane will be flying at high altitude and spot possible boats. They'll call in the coordinates to us and we'll head in that direction."

"And the rest of the time?"

"We're pretty familiar with the smugglers' favorite sea lanes. So we ply those waters and wait around to intercept them."

"And you do this during the day?"

Nodding, Noah buttered another roll. He offered it to Kit, but she shook her head. "Until about five in the afternoon. Then we head back to port. Why?"

"I'll be glad when five rolls around," Kit confided huskily.

"Don't be hard on yourself," Noah soothed. "Getting your sea legs could take several weeks."

With a pained look, Kit muttered, "What if I don't get those sea legs? I don't want to feel like this every day of the week for a year!"

"It took Joe Edwards five months before he stopped getting seasick. People adjust to sea life at different rates, Kit."

The thought of five months of this kind of feeling left Kit devastated. "You're kidding me."

"I'm not," Noah promised.

"Two weeks," Kit muttered to herself, rubbing her eyes as she sat on the edge of Noah's bunk aboard the *Osprey* after waking from her normal afternoon nap. Well, two weeks had passed and she was still miserable with seasickness every day. It was wearing badly on her. She got up shakily and put some cold water in the small basin, feeling a bit better after she'd washed her face.

Patting her face dry with the towel, she reached into the purse she kept in the drawer of Noah's desk and took out her makeup. Without it she looked positively ill. Well, wasn't she? Applying it, she noted that the blusher gave her skin a rosiness, some liquid foundation beneath her eyes erased those ever-present shadows and the lipstick made her look halfway alive.

Out of habit, Kit donned her holster and revolver. The first two weeks had been fairly routine, except for interdicting three drug-smuggling boats. Duty aboard the *Osprey* was deadly boring with intermittent moments of high tension whenever a druggie's boat was apprehended.

There was an urgent knock at the door and Kit opened it. Freddy stood there, struggling into the protective flak jacket they all wore when a boarding took place.

"Detective Anderson, we're preparing to board a ship. The skipper asked that you come to the bridge right away."

"I'll be right there, Freddy." Her heart began a slow pound, as it always did at these moments.

"Yes, ma'am!" and he ran down the narrow passageway toward the stairs.

Moments later Noah turned his attention toward the doorway. He saw the grim set of Kit's mouth as she entered the bridge. "Get your flak jacket on," he ordered. "We've got a hot-sheet yacht we're pulling over to search."

Shrugging into the heavy jacket, Kit walked over to him. Joe Edwards and the helmsman, Carter, were also on the bridge. "That's a big yacht," she commented.

"One of the biggest around. It's the *Sea Devil*," Noah said. "Do me a favor and take a look through the binoculars. See if you recognize any of the men aboard. We'll be boarding the *Sea Devil* in about ten minutes."

Her mouth grew dry as she scrutinized the four crewmen up on deck of the yacht. None of them were very savory-looking characters. As she scanned the cockpit at the rear, a gasp escaped her.

Noah frowned, focusing all his attention on Kit. She had paled considerably. "Kit?"

"My God, that's Brett Davis on board."

He watched as she placed the binoculars on the console, her eyes suddenly dark with real fear. "Davis? Who's that?"

Kit tried to control the iciness flowing through her. "Davis is a contract killer," she croaked. "He works directly for Garcia. When I was at Garcia's fortress posing as a buyer, I met him a couple of times."

Gripping her elbow, Noah guided her to the chair. He'd never seen Kit react so strongly. Wanting to put a hand on her shoulder but not daring to because of the situation, he soothed her with his voice, instead. "Take it easy. If Davis is one of Garcia's hired guns this could mean Garcia's closer to making a move to sell off his latest crop of marijuana."

Turning his attention back to the bridge, Noah ordered Edwards to prepare the boarding party. The *Sea Devil* had lowered its sail and was now heaving to as the ensign had ordered. Within minutes, the *Osprey* would dwarf the yacht as it settled alongside it. Lines would be thrown across the *Sea Devil*, mooring it to the port side of the Coast Guard vessel. Once secured, the boarding party would leap to the other deck.

Trying to think clearly, Kit watched the unfolding drama. "You're not going on board, are you?" she asked, her voice strained.

"No, it's Joe's turn."

"Thank God..." Kit whispered, and averted her eyes from Noah's sharp glance in her direction. Twice Noah had boarded boats with his team, and twice Kit had died an agonizing death, afraid that one of the smugglers might shoot instead of surrendering. No matter how many times he tried to persuade her that ninety percent of the boardings were safe, she was still left shaky in the wake of one.

"Relax," Noah urged her, taking up the portable radio. He instructed the helmsman to stop all engines, watching as the *Osprey* was brought alongside the *Sea Devil*. "Stay in here out of sight until after we've secured the situation."

Kit nodded, trying to get a grip on her rioting fears.

"Joe," Noah called on the portable radio, "keep an eye on the bearded man in the cockpit. His name is Davis, and he's one of Garcia's contract killers."

"Roger, Skipper. We'll be real careful."

Hands knotted, Kit watched from her vantage point on the bridge. Noah had moved out to the deck rail for a closer view, staying in touch with Edwards by radio. She saw Davis's square features screw up in fury as Joe cautiously approached the man, the M-16 in his hands ready to be fired.

Without realizing it, Kit got to her feet and moved quickly outside. Noah had his back to her, unaware that she was near the railing, all his attention on Davis. "Be careful, Joe..." she whispered under her breath. Davis was an angry man, yelling curses at Edwards, backing up and out of the cockpit. He refused to raise his hands above his head.

The hair on the back of Kit's neck stood on end. She turned to warn Noah that Davis wasn't going to give up without a fight. The words never left her mouth. Davis screamed a curse and pulled out a .350 Magnum from his belt, firing off a series of wild shots. The bullets whined past the bridge, burying themselves deep within the skin of the *Osprey*.

Noah lunged forward, jerking Kit to the deck to keep her from getting hit. He saw Edwards drop to the deck and fire off several more shots. In seconds the showdown was over. Davis lay on the deck, unmoving.

"Joe, get the corpsman!" he shouted over the radio. Dammit! Worriedly Noah turned his attention to Kit. She was slowly getting to her knees.

"Stay down!" he commanded harshly. Turning, he ordered several more crewmen to force all five *Sea Devil* sailors to lie on the deck, hands behind their necks. This was an armed lot, and Noah didn't want to take any more chances that they'd draw against his men.

Kit remained on the deck, breathing in gulps of warm, humid air. Her stomach turned violently, and she felt like vomiting. Had Davis killed anyone? She heard Noah's voice, crisp with authority over the radio, and she closed her eyes. Noah could have been killed—any of them could have. Shivering with apprehension, Kit lay there until Noah told her it was safe to get up.

"You okay?" Noah asked, dividing his attention between the action on the *Sea Devil* and Kit.

"Y-yes. Fine, just fine."

"I told you to stay on the bridge, dammit. Go below deck, Kit. I don't want you anywhere near the action." He glanced down at her. Her eyes were huge with horror. "Go on," he said less harshly. "We'll get this situation secured and then head back to port."

Numbly Kit nodded. "Home sounds awfully good right now," she admitted, her voice unsteady.

Kit clasped and unclasped her sweaty hands on the drive home. She was painfully aware of Noah's gaze occasionally settling on her as they drove from the pier to his house in silence. Her uniform was drenched with sweat, and she longed for a long, hot bath to unknot the kinks in her neck and shoulders.

Noah pulled into the driveway and shut off the car engine. Then he put his arm around her shoulders, noting how damp the material of her uniform was. "How you doing?"

"Okay."

He knew she was lying. Where did professional conduct begin and end? he wondered. Right now Kit needed to be held. The terror in her eyes told him everything. He sensed how close she was to exploding, five years of horror dogging her heels. Managing a slight smile for her benefit, he awkwardly patted her shoulder, then removed his arm. "Come on, let's get inside."

Kit escaped to the bathroom after greeting the animals, who met them at the door. With trembling hands, she stripped out of her uniform. Blips of past scenes involving Dante and Davis flashed through her mind. Why did this have to happen? Unable to cope with her turbulent feelings, Kit turned on the bathtub faucets and settled into the filling tub of hot water. But it was Noah's arms that she wanted around her. Kit knew that within them she would find solace. Closing her eyes, she pressed the washcloth to her face, taking in a ragged breath.

Noah had changed into a pair of jeans and a chambray shirt and was preparing to get dinner on the table. Just the nightly routine around the house had calmed his nerves. Getting shot at wasn't the norm, and as much as he himself had been shaken by the confrontation with the *Sea Devil*, he knew it had torn open a scar in Kit.

An hour passed, and he got worried when she didn't appear as she usually did after her bath. Normally Kit would come into the kitchen and help him by setting the table and making them a pot of fresh coffee. Noah had just finished preparing their individual salads, when Kit walked through the entrance. Despite her tension-lined face she looked beautiful in a pale pink cotton gown that brushed her bare feet. He'd come to look forward to her companionship in the evening, when she shed her masculine work clothes for the simple cotton gowns she wore so well.

Kit avoided Noah's searching look, going to the cabinet and pulling out the dishes to be set on the table. Her hand slipped, and one of the plates crashed to the tile floor, shattering.

With a cry Kit pressed her hand against her mouth, staring down at the broken earthenware.

Noah tensed, hearing the crash, and turned toward her. Kit stood with her back against the drain board. He walked over to her and pulled her into his arms. She was trembling, and he held her tightly against him. "It's all right," he murmured soothingly against her ear. "It's over, Kit, and you're safe." He rocked her gently, whispering words meant to heal, wanting to draw from her the fear she had carried so long by herself.

Kit collapsed against him, burying her face in the textured cotton of his shirt, longing to hide forever in his strong arms. She felt Noah's hand begin to stroke her damp hair, and she wrapped her arms around his waist, losing herself in his gentleness.

Noah's heart was beating raggedly in unison with his breathing as he pressed a kiss to her fragrant hair. Right now, Noah knew he was strong and Kit was weak. "That gun battle brought back a lot of bad memories for you, didn't it?" he asked.

Kit nodded once, realizing that their breathing was synchronizing. His arms were supportive, holding her tightly, the cranberry fabric scratchy beneath her cheek. "Y-yes."

"Want to talk about it?" Noah reluctantly loosened his embrace so he could look down at Kit. He shouldn't be holding her, because he wanted her too damn much. His body was tightening with hunger.

Fighting her own desires, Kit moved out of his arms, backing nervously away. This shouldn't have happened. None of it. Touching her brow, she stammered, "Noah, I don't feel well. I think I'll go to bed." And she fled the kitchen, hurrying down the hall toward her room before he could protest.

Dammit! Noah stood in the kitchen, staring at the entrance. He was torn between going after Kit and giving her the room she needed to work through her reaction to the shooting. Frustrated, he knelt and began retrieving the broken bits of plate. The phone rang. Rising, he picked up the kitchen extension.

"Trayhern," he growled.

"This is Cordeman."

"What do you want?"

"Considering you nabbed one of Garcia's men this afternoon, you're in a foul mood, Trayhern."

Noah gripped the receiver. "What the hell do you want, Cordeman?"

"DEA wanted me to call you and tell you that Davis is gonna make it. I imagine Kit's pretty happy about getting one of Garcia's contract gunmen."

Anger boiled up through Noah. "Kit's not happy at all," he ground out. "Seeing Davis and then getting shot at has really shattered her."

"What are you talking about?" Cordeman demanded testily. "Doesn't she realize what this means? Garcia putting one of his lieutenants like Davis in action means he's gonna make his move. That hired gun never leaves the Colombian fortress unless something big is in the offing. We figure Davis was going to meet up with Dante for future planning."

Hanging on to his temper, Noah snarled back, "I'm sure you're all pleased as hell. Kit's the one I'm worried about."

"She'll pull through for you, Trayhern. She always has in the past."

"Cordeman, this phone call is boring the hell out of me. You got anything further about Davis, you contact my commanding officer. Right now, I've had a gutful of drug-busting activity."

He slammed the receiver down, realizing how perfectly childish he probably seemed to Cordeman. But no one was worried about Kit's emotional state or frame of mind. Running his fingers through his hair, Noah returned to picking up the pieces of pottery. What should he do? Go to Kit's room and force her to talk? Or should he remain in the shadows, allowing her to come to him?

It was impossible to get their brief embrace out of his mind. Noah threw the pieces of plate into the trash. He wasn't hungry, either. Shutting off the oven, which held a casserole, he went into the living room to pour himself a drink. Perhaps later, Kit would emerge from her room and they could talk. Somehow he had to get her to trust him enough to lean on him and release all those bottled-up fears that haunted her. Somehow....

Chapter Seven

Kit was on the bridge of the *Osprey* when Joe Edwards spotted a small boat with a tattered sail on the horizon.

"Looks like a Haitian refugee boat," he said, handing Noah the binoculars.

Studying the boat for several minutes, Noah muttered, "Yeah, and not in very good shape. It's sitting low. I can see people bailing water. Let's pick them up."

"Yes, sir," and Edwards pointed the *Osprey* in that direction.

Noah set the binoculars down on the console, glancing over at Kit. Ever since the Davis shooting incident three weeks earlier, she had withdrawn deeply within herself. There were shadows beneath her haunted eyes. And nearly every night, he'd hear her get up before dawn, leave the bedroom and pad down the hall to the living room, unable to sleep. The ache in his heart intensified and so did the need to help her. Kit filled his waking, and now his sleeping, state.

Tearing from his own inner turmoil, Noah explained what was going on with the boat they would intercept shortly. "The poor of Haiti will gather on an old, leaky tub and try to make it to the U.S., hoping for a new and better life for themselves."

Kit nodded. Through her binoculars she could see the small sixteen-foot boat loaded down with human cargo, including many nearly naked children. "What will you do?"

He heard the worry in Kit's husky voice. "Let them board. Chances are, they're probably out of food, maybe even water. Depending on ocean currents and weather conditions, they may have been out to sea a good seven to ten days. Their supplies have to be running low."

Relief flowed through Kit. Nothing touched her heart like the destitute and elderly. "While I was undercover, I got a chance to work with a group of orphaned Colombian children for almost six months." Kit lowered the binoculars, searching Noah's face. He gave her strength, whether he knew it or not. "I love children. All of them."

The yearning in her voice didn't go unnoticed. "You came from a large family, so you probably want a big one yourself," he teased.

A trace of a smile crossed Kit's lips as she watched the Haitian boat drawing closer and closer. "At least three kids, maybe four."

"No basketball team?" he said, still teasing.

Drowning in Noah's warming gaze, Kit sobered. The need to walk into his arms once again to kiss him, was driving her to distraction. Tearing herself from her torrid thoughts, Kit murmured, "I love all kids. No matter what their color or nationality. They're the ones who get caught in situations beyond their control."

Noah agreed. "Well, when we get them on board, I'm sure we're going to need your help as an interpreter. They usually speak French and little else. Maybe some pidgin English, if we're lucky."

"For once I'm looking forward to our boarding a boat," Kit said fervently. Every boat they'd searched after the Davis gun incident had made her break into a sweat, her fear a palpable, living thing within her.

Noah's voice lowered with feeling. "I can tell you are."

Kit's heart went out to the fifteen Haitians in that leaky tub they called a boat. It was a miracle they hadn't sunk. She watched as Noah and his men transferred the five families to the *Osprey*. And he'd been right: the Haitians spoke little English, so she became the organizer, more or less, of getting the people comfortable.

She saw the desperation and fear in the eyes of the women as they kept asking her if they could remain in the U.S. Kit didn't know the answer. She stayed busy in the hold of the cutter while Noah was up on the bridge, placing the *Osprey* on a course for Miami. One young woman, no more than seventeen, was decidedly pregnant. Another child, Marie, hung shyly at Kit's elbow, her brown eyes huge with fear.

Getting them fed and providing space in the hold where they could rest or lie down on blankets was the main course of action. Kit crouched at the pregnant mother's side when she saw Noah enter the hold.

Noah nodded to the families, huddled in small groups. The children were far less frightened now, thanks to Kit's obvious affection and care. He halted, watching Kit as she tended to the frightened teen. Miraculously all the tension was gone from Kit's features, and her eyes were sparkling with life. He saw one little girl steal beneath Kit's left arm, snuggling close to her.

Kit looked at Noah when he knelt opposite her. His eyes were warm with pleasure. "Looks like you've already got a family," he noted, motioning to the little girl in Kit's arms.

Embracing Marie, Kit nodded. "She sort of took to me, I guess."

Moved because she had shared her feelings with him, Noah realized the child was drawing Kit out of her shell. "Anyone in their right mind would," Noah admitted, a catch in his voice. And when he saw the surprise in Kit's eyes, he quickly changed the subject. "You can tell these people that we'll be taking them to Miami, not back to Haiti. Immigration will see that they're given food and shelter. There's a good chance they'll be staying in the U.S.''

Tears surged into Kit's eyes unexpectedly. Embarrassed that Noah had seen them, she wiped them away with the back of her hand. "That's wonderful," she whispered in a strained voice. "They were all so fearful you were going to return them to Haiti. Let me tell them."

Noah got to his feet, watching hope spring up to the faces of the refugees as Kit told them the happy news. It made him feel good. In his daily life he often saw only negativity. This time there was something positive, and he relished the Haitians' reactions to Kit's announcement. He frowned, noticing that tears continued to stream down Kit's face. She placed Marie beside her mother and turned to him.

"I—I have to pull myself together, Noah. May I use your cabin for just a—"

"Come with me," he told her huskily, putting his hand on her elbow and leading her down the passageway. She was trembling.

"I'll be okay," Kit stammered, trying to stem the flow of tears. Why was she crying like this? Why couldn't she stop? Noah's firm touch on her arm only made her want to cry more. Blinded by the onslaught of tears, Kit didn't try to pull out of his grasp.

"Hang on," Noah said, opening the door to his cabin. He drew her inside, guiding her to the bunk, where she sat down. Picking up the phone, he called the bridge and told Edwards to take command for now. When he turned back to her, she was hunched over, hands clasped in her lap, head bowed. Removing his officer's cap he placed it on the desk, then crouched in front of her. The instant his hands came to rest on her slumped shoulders, a sob tore from her.

"Oh, Noah . . ."

He maintained a firm grip on her arms. "It's about time," he said thickly.

More sobs punished her, and Kit raised her head. Noah's face was nothing but a blur. "Wh-what are you talking about?"

"You're burned out, Kit. And you've been holding a lot of ugly stuff inside you." He pushed a wayward strand of hair behind her ear. "I've been waiting and wondering when you were going to let it all go." His voice grew dark. "Don't fight it. I'm here, and I'll help you."

She hadn't cried in almost a year. Kit clung to his tender gaze, feeling as if she were coming apart from the inside out. Just the husky tenor of Noah's voice dissolved the last of the barriers that held her grief and fear captive. Noah rose and sat down on the bunk beside Kit, opening his arms, drawing her to him.

As she sank against him, Noah groaned, wrapping his arms tightly about her, rocking her gently, as if she were a hurt child. "It's okay, Kit, let it out, let it all go...." And he shut his eyes, pressing his cheek against her hair, allowing her to weep freely. Her fingers dug deeply into his chest, and Noah rubbed her shoulders and back, willing out the horror she'd held so long in abeyance.

```
*******************************************************
*  You may have already won a lifetime of cash payments *
*  totaling up to $1,000,000.00!  Play our Sweepstakes  *
*  Game--Here's how it works...                         *
*******************************************************
```

Each of the first three tickets has a unique Sweepstakes number. If your Sweepstakes numbers match any of the winning numbers selected by our computer, you could win the amount shown under the gold rub-off on that ticket.

Using an eraser, rub off the gold boxes on tickets #1-3 to reveal how much each ticket could be worth if it is a winning ticket. You must return the <u>entire</u> card to be eligible. (See official rules in the back of this book for details.)

At the same time you play your tickets for big cash prizes, Silhouette also invites you to participate in a special trial of our Reader Service by accepting one or more FREE book(s) from Silhouette Special Edition.® To request your free book(s), just rub off the gold box on ticket #4 to reveal how many free book(s) you will receive.

When you receive your free book(s), we hope you'll enjoy them and want to see more. So unless we hear from you, every month we'll send you 6 additional Silhouette Special Edition® novels. Each book is yours to keep for only $2.74* each--21¢ less per book than the cover price! There are <u>no</u> additional charges for shipping and handling and of course, you may cancel Reader Service privileges at any time by marking "cancel" on your shipping statement or returning an unopened shipment of books to us at our expense. Either way your shipments will stop. You'll receive no more books; you'll have no further obligation.

PLus—you get a FREE MYSTERY GIFT!

If you return your game card with **<u>all four gold boxes</u>** rubbed off, you will also receive a FREE Mystery Gift. It's your **immediate reward** for sampling your free book(s), **and** it's yours to keep no matter what you decide.

P.S.

Remember, the first set of one or more book(s) is FREE. So rub off the gold box on ticket #4 and return the entire sheet of tickets today!

*Terms and prices subject to change without notice.
 Sales taxes applicable in New York and Iowa.

"GIVE YOUR HEART TO SILHOUETTE" SWEEPSTAKES

DETACH HERE AND RETURN ENTIRE SHEET OF TICKETS NOW!

#1 **$1,000,000.00**
Rub off to reveal potential value if this is a winning ticket: ►

UNIQUE
SWEEPSTAKES
NUMBER: 6B 991810

#2 **$1,000,000.00**
Rub off to reveal potential value if this is a winning ticket: ►

UNIQUE
SWEEPSTAKES
NUMBER: 7B 993795

#3 **$1,000,000.00**
Rub off to reveal potential value if this is a winning ticket: ►

UNIQUE
SWEEPSTAKES
NUMBER: 8B 991461

#4 **ONE OR MORE FREE BOOKS**
HOW MANY FREE BOOKS?
Rub off to reveal number of free books you will receive ►

1672765559

Yes! Enter my sweepstakes numbers in the Sweepstakes and let me know if I've won a cash prize. If gold box on ticket **#4** is rubbed off, I will also receive one or more Silhouette Special Edition® novels as a FREE tryout of the Reader Service, along with a FREE Mystery Gift as explained on the opposite page.   235 CIS R1X4

NAME

ADDRESS   APT.

CITY   STATE   ZIP CODE

DON'T FORGET...

... Return this card today with ticket #4 rubbed off, and receive 4 free books and a free mystery gift.

... You will receive books well before they're available in stores and at a discount off cover prices.

... No obligation to buy. You can cancel at any time by writing "cancel" on your statement or returning an unopened shipment to us at our cost.

BUSINESS REPLY CARD

First Class   Permit No. 717   Buffalo, NY

Postage will be paid by addressee

Silhouette Reader Service™

MILLION DOLLAR SWEEPSTAKES

901 Fuhrmann Blvd.
P.O. Box 1867
Buffalo, N.Y. 14240-9952

NO POSTAGE
NECESSARY
IF MAILED
IN THE
UNITED STATES

Every stroke of his fingers on her back took a little more of the pain away from her. Kit surrendered her trust to him, something she'd never done with a man before. She felt Noah move slightly, his strong, sensual mouth pressed against her temple in a soothing kiss. Kit instinctively nuzzled upward, finding refuge in the feathery touch of his mouth. A soft moan of surrender slid from her as he barely grazed her mouth.

Giving free rein to his feelings for Kit, Noah cradled her chin, imprisoning her. He leaned down to kiss those full, glistening lips, and tasted the bitterness of salt on her flesh. A fire lit explosively within him. She was soft and inviting.... He grazed her lips with his tongue, and his body tightened with desire as he molded his mouth hungrily to hers. At first there was no response from Kit, but he continued his gentle seduction. And then her lips moved shyly against his, sending a soaring sheet of flame through him. He felt the hunger of wanting to love her physically gnaw at him. But his heart instructed him differently.

Body hard and throbbing, Noah tore his mouth from hers. Kit was breathing raggedly. He saw wonder and some unknown feeling in her wide, gray eyes. She was just as shocked by his kiss as he was.

The silence eddied around them. Kit drowned in Noah's turbulent green gaze. She read so much in his eyes, a richness of feelings that flowed through her like a gentle wind in the wake of a destructive storm. Kit swallowed hard, unwilling to leave Noah's embrace. The unsure smile that tipped the corners of his mouth endeared him to her even more.

"All right now?" he asked, his voice little more than a rasp. His senses were vibrantly alive because of her, because of everything she was and was not. She had been so sweet and feminine in his arms. Noah knew his kiss had not been out of pity for her condition. Just the lustrous quality in her eyes sent him reeling. He had to get up and leave. He had to staunch the flow of this molten ribbon that so powerfully connected them.

"Y-yes, fine…" Kit whispered. She tried to wipe her cheeks dry but didn't succeed very well. "I feel so stupid, breaking down like that for no reason."

"Don't you think it was good to cry and get rid of all that poison inside you?"

Sniffing, Kit couldn't meet his gaze. But his deep voice was a balm to her ravaged state. "I guess so, Noah."

"Maybe you'll be able to sleep better at night from now on."

Stunned that he knew of her nightly wakenings, Kit stared up at him. His eyes were gentle with understanding.

"I haven't met too many agents who didn't have some sleepless nights," Noah said soothingly. "From now on, if you need a shoulder to cry on, look me up."

Taking a deep breath, Kit nodded. "I will."

"Promise?"

"Promise."

Noah rose—the last thing he wanted to do. Keeping a hand on her shoulder, he said, "Stay here awhile and work through the rest of it, Kit. Okay?"

She lowered her lashes, her heart squeezing with fresh pain. Noah was retreating rapidly. His voice had taken on that familiar authoritative quality. "I'll be fine," she promised in a rasp. "Go ahead, I know you have things to attend to."

The disappointment in her tone was very real. Noah wondered why, but didn't ask. Reluctantly he allowed his hand to slide from her shoulder. "I'll see you later."

The door shut quietly, and Kit looked up. All her senses focused on the wonderful kiss they had shared. It had been so unexpected, but so right. Getting up, Kit ran some water in the small basin and washed her flushed face, hoping to get rid of the signs of crying. What she couldn't wash away was Noah's tenderness or her physical need to love him.

As she dried her face with a towel, she tried to understand what had happened. Ever since she'd met Noah, some undefinable tension had simmered hotly between them. And every day it seemed to heighten, making her excruciatingly aware of being a woman. All these feelings were new and disturbing.

Placing the towel on the bracket, Kit took in a deep breath, trying to steady her roiling emotions. Nothing worked. She sat back down, burying her face in her hands. A young Haitian child had broken through the barriers behind which she had hidden so many old hurts and griefs from past wounds. Somehow Noah had known what was happening and taken her aside so that he could hold her while she worked through that terrible storm of feelings. But he didn't have to kiss her. And she didn't have to respond, either. Kit's eyes grew troubled with the implications. They had to work together, and this shouldn't be happening.

If she was any judge of the situation, Noah was just as surprised by the kiss as she was. But both of them had wanted it, needed it. Kit tried to tell herself that Noah had kissed her out of compassion, nothing else. There could be nothing else between them right now. Her entire life was focused on trying to collar Garcia.

Rising, Kit studied herself in the mirror. Her eyes were a soft gray color, her mouth still tingling in the aftermath of Noah's kiss. She saw none of the old Kit Anderson left as she searched the face in front of her. In the past month Noah had brought out her vulnerability. And as the tides of the ocean ebbed and flowed because of the moon's pull, she was responding in kind to him.

"You've got to get a hold on yourself," she whispered. It was Friday. Thank God Alyssa Trayhern would be visiting this weekend. Kit felt incredibly susceptible after Noah's kiss. She had no idea how she would behave if they had to spend this weekend alone together. Yes, Aly's presence was essential.

"Aly!" Noah grinned and threw his arms around his tall, slender sister. He hugged her fiercely, laughing as she wrapped her arms around him.

"Oh, Noah." Aly sighed, standing back and looking up at him. "It's so *good* to see a friendly face. I'm sorry I'm early, but I had to escape from Pensacola for a while or lose what little's left of my mind."

"Friendly and glad that you're here. Come on in."
Noah ushered his younger sister inside. It was eight in
the morning, and Aly was right on time. She was
dressed in a short-sleeved bright green blouse that
emphasized her auburn hair, and a pair of khaki-
colored slacks. And she looked very tired. Almost as
tired as Kit.

Aly leaned down to pet Tripoli, then gave each of
the cats a ruffle on the head before following Noah
from the foyer.

"You're just in time for breakfast, sis. I was fixing
some of my world-famous Trayhern omelets."

Chuckling, Aly followed her brother into the
kitchen. "Noah, my stomach isn't up to a wild ome-
let today."

"I'll make you a tame one, then. Fair enough? Sit
down. Coffee?"

Placing her purse on another chair, Aly nodded. "A
stiff drink would be more like it."

"That bad at Pensacola, huh?" Noah handed her
the cup and returned to his cooking.

"That bad." Aly looked around. "Hey, you said
you had a roommate. Where is she?"

With a grimace Noah turned and faced his sister. "I
couldn't say much on the phone when you called last
week, Aly. She isn't exactly a roommate."

Aly raised an eyebrow, her eyes sparkling. "Been a
long time since you had a serious relationship, if my
memory serves me correctly."

Stirring the egg mixture, Noah muttered, "It's not
what you think."

Aly tittered delightfully, and sat back in the chair, enjoying Noah's sudden discomfort. "Oh...okay. Tell me all about her."

"There's not much to tell. Detective Kit Anderson is here on police business I can't talk too much about. This is a safe house for her."

Aly frowned. "A safe house?"

Noah set the bowl on the drain board and added a number of vegetables, then some shredded cheese to the mixture. "Yeah. There's a Mob contract out on her, and everyone concerned felt she'd be better off here."

"My God, Noah, that's dangerous! This is something new. I mean, I've heard of taking work home with you, but isn't this going too far?"

Chuckling, Noah said, "Don't overreact. Being a safe house isn't really all that dangerous."

"What's she like?"

"Kit is . . ." Noah struggled with adjectives. If he allowed his heart to talk, he'd say that she was incredibly beautiful, with eyes that shone like the ocean touched with moonlight. That ever since the kiss yesterday, there had been a new unsureness between them.

"Yes?" Aly goaded, watching her brother's face closely.

"She's been an undercover agent for the narc division for five years." There, that was a safe, impersonal comment. "Kit should be joining us shortly for breakfast."

"Great. Frankly, I need a family situation to un-wind from that murderous flight school."

He gave her a dark look as he poured the first ome-let into the skillet. "It's not a family situation be-tween me and Kit, Aly."

She grinned at his defensiveness. "Okay, big brother, anything you say. But I see that look in your eye, and I hear it in your voice."

Heat flowed into Noah's cheeks, and he was acutely aware of Aly's appraisal. She sat there with a silly know-it-all grin on her face. He had never been able to hide much from his sister. "You're barking up the wrong tree," he growled unhappily.

Kit entered the kitchen, dressed in a pale pink blouse and a pair of threadbare jeans. She halted, seeing a red-headed woman at the table. It had to be Alyssa. Grateful for her presence even though she really didn't know her, Kit gave her a warm smile. "You must be Alyssa," she said, moving to the table and extending her hand.

Aly rose, shaking her hand. "And you're Kit Anderson. Call me Aly. It's good to meet you." She shot a glance over at Noah, who had his back to them. "My brother has been telling me all about you," she said in a conspiratorial tone.

Uncomfortable, Noah turned and gave his sister a warning look. "You'd better explain yourself, Aly. And in a hurry."

Aly sat there, a pleased look on her face, deliber-ately ignoring Noah's remarks.

Kit poured herself a cup of coffee, vibrantly aware of Noah only a few feet away from where she stood. He looked magnificent in a forest green polo shirt and faded jeans. And when he glanced in her direction to mutter "Good morning," her heart squeezed, then began to pound.

"Good morning," she murmured in return, retreating hastily to the table, where Aly sat.

"I understand you're in navy flight school," Kit began, trying to move to a safe topic of conversation, aware that Aly had a special look of alertness in her startling blue eyes. She was very pretty, Kit thought, taking in the cute pixie-style cut of Aly's auburn hair that emphasized the fine qualities of her facial features. Kit liked her immediately. There was a tension to Aly, as if she were a clock that had been wound too tightly. Her movements were quick, concise and sure, shouting her obvious confidence.

"Yes, I'm battling my way through Pensacola," she griped good-naturedly.

Noah placed a plate in front of Kit. "This one's for you," he said.

Kit looked down at the omelet, hash browns and toast, distraught at the quantity of food. "Noah—"

"Looks like he's trying to fatten you up," Aly noted wryly, then added, "Noah has this thing about always helping out the underdogs of the world. If you're too skinny, he wants to fatten you up. If you've got a problem, he'll loan you his shoulder to cry on. If you need a place to hide, he'll throw open the doors to his home." She smiled warmly over at Kit. "He takes in stray animals, too, as you can see.'' She gestured at the two cats and dog sitting patiently around the table, waiting for scraps.

Kit lowered her lashes, unable to stop a smile. "Yes, Noah helps people and animals in many ways."

"Here, eat this and quit talking," Noah muttered to his sister, putting a plate in front of her.

"You must think I'm skinny, too," Aly teased, picking up the fork.

"You both are."

"Uh-oh, watch it, Kit. My brother is stalking us. If we keep eating like this, we'll balloon to a hundred and thirty in no time."

Laughter spilled from Kit. She was delighted with Aly's quick retorts. Noah was terribly uncomfortable, and if she wasn't mistaken, that dull red color on his cheeks meant he was blushing. Suddenly, with Alyssa's effervescent presence, the weekend was taking on a wonderful new quality.

"So, what's on the agenda for the rest of the day?" Aly wanted to know after breakfast.

Noah didn't like the way Aly was watching him— especially whenever he talked with Kit. It was only polite table conversation, but she was far too interested to suit him. She obviously thought there was something between them, when there wasn't. He was about ready to throttle her. "*I* was going to work in the garage on that bureau I started building three months ago. I've got some sanding to do on it before

I start rubbing it down to bring out the highlights in the wood.''

''And I was going to weed the flower beds,'' Kit said, rising to clear the plates from the table.

''What a homey twosome you are.''

Noah glared at Aly, but said nothing.

''Tell you what, Kit,'' Aly began with enthusiasm, ''I want to catch up on what my handsome brother has been doing, and later I'll help you weed. It's about time I did penance in the form of ground duty.''

Kit grinned. ''Sounds good. There are enough weeds for both of us.''

Chuckling, Aly followed Noah out of the house to the garage. She placed her hand on his shoulder. ''She's really beautiful, Noah.''

He opened the garage door, and sunlight spilled into the gloomy depths. ''Just what the hell were you trying to do in there, Aly?'' he demanded, walking over to the chest of drawers he'd fashioned out of cherry wood.

''What?''

He sized up his spunky sister. ''You know damn well what.''

Aly picked up some sandpaper and handed it to Noah. ''Come on, Noah! I'd have to be blind not to see you like her.''

He snorted and sat down to begin sanding the wood. ''You're way off base.''

Kneeling and starting to sand the other side of the bureau, Aly muttered, ''Noah, you never could hide a thing from me. So don't sit there and tell me you don't like Kit Anderson! I can see it in your eyes and the way you talk to her.''

''You're nuts.''

Tittering, Aly caught his glance. ''Your voice gets soft when you speak to her, Noah.''

''Why don't you just sand, and we'll talk about something else.''

''How long have you known Kit?''

''A month.''

''She married?''

''No.''

''A boyfriend?''

''Dammit, no! Can we get on another topic?''

''No. Hey, I like Kit! She may be a cop, but there's a special quality about her.''

He sanded with more intensity, refusing to look over at his sister. ''Yeah, she is special,'' he grumbled.

''See?''

''Shut up and keep working.''

Laughing delightedly, Aly did as she was told for about five minutes. Breaking the pleasant silence, she asked, ''How can Kit take that kind of dangerous pressure?''

The scowl on Noah's forehead deepened. ''That's what I've been wanting to know myself. Frankly, I thing she took up police work because her family's like ours—bound by tradition.''

''Oh, I see. Several generations of cops, huh?''

''Yeah.'' Noah wiped off the sweat gathering above his upper lip and concentrated with renewed vigor on the bureau. He wished with all his might that his eternally nosy sister would drop the subject. "Kit isn't cut out for police work. Never has been. Yesterday she broke—" Noah caught himself. Dammit, he never meant to talk to anyone about that! He saw Aly's eyes grow gentle.

"What do mean, 'broke'?"

"Forget I said it."

"No." Aly reached out and gripped his arm. "Noah, it's obvious to me you care an awful lot for Kit. Come on, I'm your sister. If you can't talk to me, who can you talk to?"

Noah sat back, staring down at the sandpaper in his dusty hands. "Kit has been carrying a lot of past grief and terror in her from her years as an undercover agent," he said finally. "Yesterday we picked up a bunch of Haitian refugees, and it got to her." He sighed, staring out the opened door of the garage. "There was one little girl who absolutely adored Kit. When I went below to check on everyone, she had the girl in her arms. Kit was acting as interpreter, and I told her to tell the group they would be going to Miami."

"And then?" Aly stopped sanding and watched her brother's face intently.

"Once they understood they would be going to the U.S., the people started to cry and thank Kit. She started crying with them. And then she couldn't stop, so I took her to my cabin for some privacy."

"She was finally letting go? Getting it out of her system?" Aly guessed.

Noah nodded, exhaling. "Yeah..."

"Something else happened?" Aly pressed gently.

He folded the sandpaper methodically in his hand. "Something happened," Noah admitted heavily. "She felt so good in my arms. It was like a shock to me, Aly."

"What was a shock?"

Noah compressed his mouth into a thin line, looking over at his sister. "I kissed her."

Brows arching, Aly grinned. "What's so shocking about that? Kissing's pretty natural and normal between a man and a woman."

"Smart ass."

Swallowing her smile, Aly asked, "Did you do it out of pity, because she needed help?"

"No. I don't know…" He snorted. "I don't know much of anything right now with Kit around. I've got a job to do, and I'm supposed to be professional about all this. Kit's on the *Osprey* with me five days a week. And then she lives here."

"Kinda close quarters with each other all the time, huh?"

With a curt nod Noah returned to the job of sanding the bureau. "Very close."

"I see."

"I wish to hell I did. That kiss came out of nowhere, Aly. I haven't been thinking about Kit in those terms."

She began to sand again, watching Noah closely. "Maybe you were, but weren't aware of it."

"We came together like an explosion. I've never been so shaken, Aly. And I've had my fair share of relationships. Kissing a woman isn't something new to me.''

"Kit is different."

"She sure as hell is."

With a smile, Aly reached over and patted her brother on the shoulder. "Hang in there. I have a hunch all this will become crystal clear to you after a while."

Noah wasn't so sure. He hadn't been able to forget, much less erase, the kiss he'd shared so hotly with Kit. All night he'd tossed and turned in bed, replaying that molten moment. her mouth had been so soft and inviting, and he'd drowned in her arms for that one stunning moment torn out of time. In a monumental effort to put Kit out of his mind, Noah changed the subject to Aly's progress at flight school. She complied, telling him about the instructor who was trying to wash her out because she was the sister of a traitor.

It was almost noon when Aly finished talking about the incidents at Pensacola. The bureau had been sanded, and now needed a second sanding with a finer grit. "Why don't you go help Kit for a while?" Noah suggested, standing and brushing the dust from his jeans.

"Better yet, I'm thirsty. How about if I make us all some lemonade and bring it out to you and her?"

"Sounds great. Thanks."

Kit was on her hands and knees when Aly came out the front door, bearing two glasses of lemonade. Kit smiled gratefully, sitting back on her heels.

"I was dying of thirst. How did you know?" Kit said, taking the glass. "Thanks."

"I was getting thirsty out there in the garage, so I figured you were probably even thirstier working out here in the sun." Aly sat down on the grass, admiring the flowers.

"I'm taking a break." Kit motioned to the border surrounding the front of the house. "Got half of it weeded so far."

"I'll help you with the second half."

Sipping the sweet, ice-cold lemonade, Kit groaned with satisfaction. "This tastes wonderful." She wiped the sweat off her forehead with the back of her arm. "You're a mind reader like Noah."

"Oh?"

Kit smiled over at Aly, who sat cross-legged in front of her. "He's forever surprising me with his ability to know what someone needs."

Aly sipped the lemonade and nodded. "Noah's always had a special sensitivity to everyone around him." She pursed her lips, holding Kit's friendly gaze. "I imagine working and living together is a bit of a strain on you."

Absently Kit picked at a few weeds between the marigolds. "In some ways," she admitted. "I feel I've become a real burden to him."

Snorting, Aly stretched out on her stomach. "You're the best thing that's happened to him, Kit."

"I find that hard to believe."

Choosing a blade of grass, Aly put it in her mouth and chewed on it thoughtfully. "I'm sure he told you about Morgan and what happened."

"Yes. Knowing you and Noah, I find it hard to believe that your brother would be capable of such an act."

"Exactly. Morgan didn't defect, and he didn't leave his men to die alone on that hill." She grimaced. "That aside, the past five years have been hell on all our family. Noah got it broadside because he was already an officer in the Coast Guard. A lot of people went out of their way to try to derail his career because they thought Morgan was a traitor and they wanted to punish a Trayhern for it. Noah became their target."

"I understand you've had your share of hell with that particular item, too," Kit said, noting the pain in Aly's eyes.

"Yeah, nobody escaped the full-scale attack by the press and Pentagon," she muttered bitterly. "Because of it, Noah's had to double his efforts to keep his record clean. He's had to become like Superman and overachieve just to be grudgingly accepted by his superiors. I'd hate to add up all the overtime and special assignments he's taken to keep our name clean and his nose out of trouble."

Kit frowned, weaving invisible patterns in the short grass where she sat. "You mean he isn't really a workaholic?"

"No. Have you seen his carpentry out in the garage?"

"Yes, he showed it to me one time. There are some beautiful but unfinished pieces of furniture out there."

"Precisely. Noah's been good with woodworking since he was in his teens. At one time he wanted to be a wood craftsman."

"But family priorities got in the way?" Kit guessed.

"Bingo. Before Morgan disappeared and this whole mess erupted, Noah had his life laid out. He likes the Coast Guard, but loved his woodworking even more. I remember he and I used to talk about his dreams."

"What dreams?" Kit asked softly, seeing Noah in a new, more positive light.

"Oh, you know." Aly rolled over on her back, closing her eyes and absorbing the warmth of the July sunlight. "He wanted to make his living doing woodworking. And he wanted a wife who wanted lots of kids, because he loves kids."

A lump formed in Kit's throat, and she stared down at the grass. "But then family obligations got in the way."

"Noah figured he'd put in the mandatory twenty years, retire, then pursue his real dream." Aly opened one eye and looked over at Kit. "Of course, he wanted to marry and have that passel of kids before that."

"I see . . ." Kit said faintly.

"Funny how family tradition can change things," Aly went on quietly. "I mean, I love the navy, and even more, I love to fly. Noah wasn't really in love with the military the way Morgan and I were. That's why he joined the Coast Guard."

"Because it's the least militaristic?"

"Right. He's always been good at helping others, and felt the Coast Guard was a perfect answer for him. They do a lot of rescue work, and he's happy in that capacity."

With a sigh, Kit got to her knees and began to pick at the weeds once again. "It looks like we've both been trapped by tradition."

"Noah said he didn't feel you belonged in police work."

"He's right. I wish I'd known that five years earlier."

Aly slowly got up and came over to join Kit at weeding. "I think being here with Noah is going to be good for you," she confided. "Let him take care of you. It's what he's best at." A smile filtered through Aly's serious demeanor. "Right now, you need a little attention and care. And Noah needs someone to care for."

Chapter Eight

"Thank God it's Friday and we've got the weekend ahead of us," Kit said, meaning it as she climbed into Noah's Trans Am. Behind them, the *Osprey* sat docked in the shadowy dusk.

Noah gave her a quick glance while buckling up. "Ever since Aly visited, all hell has broken loose for us," he griped. Driving slowly down the parking lot, Noah took off his officer's cap, tossing it in the back seat.

"Three weeks of incredible work," Kit added tiredly. "I really think Garcia's deluging U.S. shores with boats to get our attention so he can make his big drop elsewhere without law enforcement interference."

"I think you're right." Noah turned the car onto the street, heading for the on-ramp to the freeway that would take them home. The *Osprey* had intercepted at least two boats a day. It was as if someone were sending them in droves toward the Florida coast. His and Kit's days started before dawn and rarely ended before nine or ten at night.

Kit leaned back and chuckled. "I don't know if we want Aly to visit this Saturday, Noah. She was the harbinger of all this boat activity," she teased.

Grinning, Noah nodded. "I'll tell her it's all her fault." His eyes darkened. "Are you sure you don't mind if she visits us again?"

"Of course not. I like your sister." Aly had been the perfect buffer between Kit and Noah, easing the tension between them. Kit didn't want to admit that living with him was like a wonderful dream come true. It was as if they were married—without the physical intimacy.

"She thinks an awful lot of you, too." Noah studied Kit's face in the light and darkness for a moment. Ever since she had cried in his arms, she had changed markedly for the better. No longer did she get up at night to pace the house. The shadows were almost gone from beneath her sparkling eyes, and she smiled more often. With a monumental effort Noah returned to the task of driving. Kit's mouth was far too delicious, and there was too much danger in thinking about the one kiss they'd shared.

Yawning, Kit muttered, "I don't know about you, but I'm dead on my feet. As soon as we get home, I'm going to have a bath and go to bed."

"Good idea, because I'm sure Aly will show up bright and early on our doorstep tomorrow morning," Noah said with a chuckle.

"She's good for us. We need a laugh or two," Kit returned with a smile. A feathery feeling tremored through her as Noah said "our" doorstep. The past few weeks had bound them inexorably to each other in simple but telling ways. And she knew without a doubt that Noah wasn't really like Pete at all. Leaning back, she closed her eyes, looking forward to Aly's effervescent visit. Yes, they all needed to laugh, kick up their heels and have a good time.

"Psst, Kit!" Aly leaned forward from where she sat on the couch with Noah, a bowl of popcorn in hand.

Kit roused herself from the floor, where she lay on her stomach. They were watching a movie on television together on a Saturday night. "What?" She saw the look of devilry in Aly's eyes.

Aly set her bowl of popcorn aside. "Did you know that my brother is ticklish?"

Before Kit could respond, Aly stretched across the couch and began tickling Noah unmercifully beneath the arm. Thoroughly engrossed in the movie and oblivious to their banter, he let out a yelp of surprise.

Kit sat up, watching the popcorn Noah had held in his bowl go flying all over the couch and carpet. Aly pressed her attack, tickling Noah until he fell off the couch and onto the floor.

"There!" Aly crowed triumphantly, getting to her feet with a grin. She beamed at her brother, who was still laughing from his prone position on the carpet.

"What was that for?" Noah demanded, sitting up and grinning, too.

"Things were getting too quiet around here," Aly announced. "I'm going to get some soda pop. Anyone want some?"

Noah looked around with dismay at the scattered popcorn. "We drank it all."

"Then I'll drive down to the corner store and get us some more," Aly said. "Be back in a bit, gang. Kit, why don't you help Noah pick up all the popcorn he spilled?"

Giggling, Kit crawled over on her hands and knees to where Noah sat. She began to pick up the popcorn, one piece at a time, putting it back in the emptied bowl. Both Calico and Tuna Boat were getting their share before she could rescue all the kernels.

Noah scowled at her. "What's so funny, Ms. Anderson?"

"Nothing," she said, giving him a merry look. "Big, bad old Coast Guard officer is reduced to Jell-O by his teeny little sister..." and she started laughing so hard she had to hold her hand to her stomach.

A mischievous grin spread across Noah's face. He heard Aly close the door on her way out. "It's a good thing we're alone," he growled, and then lunged at Kit.

Startled, Kit let out a yelp and tried to escape, but Noah pinned her to the carpet, anchoring her hands above her head. "Noah!" she gasped. His body was so close to hers.

"Let's see what a big, bad police detective does under the same circumstances," he threatened as he began to tickle her ribs.

A cry broke from Kit, and she curled up, laughing hysterically. It was impossible to get away from Noah, and all she could do was try to protect her sensitive rib cage from his attack. Finally tears were streaming down her cheeks.

"Uncle! Uncle!" she gasped, giggling. Kit placed a hand against his chest, wildly aware of his masculinity. Noah's face loomed close, and she could feel the warmth of his breath fanning across her cheek. "I give... I give..." she pleaded breathlessly.

Capturing Kit's hands once again above her head, Noah straddled her with his body. "Uncle, huh?" he gasped, smiling down at her. God, but she was beautiful, her eyes lustrous with happiness. Taking his hand, he smoothed several strands of hair from her eyes.

Kit's breasts rose and fell rapidly. Noah was so close that she could feel the heat from his body. Although he had captured her, he wasn't hurting her. Far from it. Kit drowned in his sea-colored eyes. The memory of his kiss flowed to the surface of her heart and mind.

Noah saw her lips part provocatively as she held his gaze. This need for her was excruciating, her slender form taut beneath his. "Next weekend," he rasped, "I want you to come with me."

Puzzled, Kit asked, "What's so special about next weekend?" His fingers traced her brow and a tiny shiver arched through her.

"We both need a rest from work," he decided. "I want to take you to a special place for a day." Tightening his hold on her wrists, Noah allowed his other hand to drop threateningly to her rib cage. "And if you don't agree, Ms. Anderson, I'm going to tickle the daylights out of you."

A breathy laugh escaped her. "If you start tickling me again, Noah Trayhern, I'm going to wet my pants and you know it!"

He gloated, his gaze never leaving her soft, sparkling eyes. He wanted to drown himself in their depths. "Then agree to be pirated away for a day."

It was impossible to relax beneath him. The urge to lean upward and touch his mobile mouth was too much for Kit to ignore. Everything about Noah excited her, and she inhaled his special scent, closing her eyes. "I'll go. Anything not to be tickled."

"Good." Noah released her wrists and forced himself to move off her. Kit was too enticing, too close, and he could feel heat building in himself. He knelt at her side and helped her sit up.

Giving him a wary look, Kit ran her fingers through her short hair. A tremor of longing sang through her as she sat next to him. "Where are you taking me?"

"It's a surprise," he replied enigmatically. "One that you deserve."

"I don't believe this is happening," Kit muttered, trading a glance with Noah as he drove.

His smile was one of pure devastation. "Just one of life's little bonuses. How could I possibly leave Tripoli behind while we enjoy this special Saturday?"

Tripoli hung his head between the seats, panting to emphasize the point. Kit stifled her laughter, shaking her head. "We're going on your boat with a dog!"

He shrugged his broad shoulders, the white polo shirt he had on emphasizing their breadth. "Sit back and relax. This is our day to enjoy."

Kit ran her fingers through her black hair, smiling. When Noah had confided that he was going to take her out on his boat to a beautiful cove for a picnic, she had been excited. He'd promised her it would be a short trip by water, knowing that she would get seasick as always.

She curled up on the seat, rested her chin on her arm and watched Noah. "If I didn't know better, I'd say Tripoli is looking forward to our outing."

Noah grinned, guiding the car slowly down the quay toward a small bay that sheltered over a hundred privately owned boats and yachts. "He should. Every time I get a chance, I take him with me."

"And he likes boating?"

"Why not? In the days of sailing ships, they used to carry cats on board to catch rats. Why not a dog?"

"I certainly hope you're not hinting there are rats aboard your boat!"

Noah laughed, his green eyes flecked with gold as he looked over at her. "Trust me. Tripoli has sea legs and he isn't with us to chase rats."

"I wish I had sea legs," Kit complained, "so I would quit getting sick every day on the *Osprey*."

Noah lost some of his merriment. "I guess you're just one of those people with an inner ear imbalance, who will never adjust to sea life." He brightened. "But we'll take a swim, catch some fish and have a fine time on the beach."

"Remember, I'm not such a hot swimmer, either, Noah."

"Trust me. I won't let anything happen to you."

"That's what they all say—'trust me.'"

Noah grinned. "If you fall overboard, I'll just toss Tripoli in the water with a rope in his mouth. He'll keep you afloat until I can reach you."

"Very funny," Kit growled.

The boat basin looked like the others she had seen dotting the coastline of Florida. The sun was hot, the August day humid, with rapidly building cumulus clouds budding into towering turrets to the west of them. Kit wore her pale lavender bathing suit with a pair of comfortable pink shorts.

Carrying a small picnic basket, Kit watched as Tripoli bounced happily around them as they walked down the wooden wharf. Despite her misgivings about being on the boat, Kit felt her fear begin to fade as she allowed the pleasant events of the day to take their course. The past week had been just as busy as the three before. And Noah was right: they needed to take a breath and relax.

Noah halted and nodded to the boat on the right. "Meet the *Rainbow*."

Kit's gaze roved appreciatively over the eighteen-foot cabin cruiser. How like Noah to name his boat the *Rainbow*. His entire life-style attested to the fact that he allowed few stormy days to inhibit his mood. Noah crossed the plankway, then held out his hand for her.

"Okay, you're next, landlubber."

Kit returned his infectious smile, gripped his hand and stepped aboard. "It's a beautiful vessel, Noah."

"Coming from you, that's quite a compliment. Climb up this small ladder and get comfortable by the helm. I'm going to cast off."

She ascended the ladder to the bridge. Two black leather chairs were bolted to the deck on either side of the wheel. Kit sat down, glancing around until Noah gingerly came up the ladder. He looked breathtakingly masculine in a pair of well-worn cutoffs. Pulling off his shirt, he set it to one side and then took the wheel. Pressing the button on the console, he brought the motors to life with a throaty growl. A slight vibration raced through the sleek craft. Noah guided them safely out of the harbor, the turquoise water beckoning, adding to Kit's building excitement. She tried to ignore the rich brown tone of his upper body as he steered them out into the beautiful waters, heading south.

"I'm jealous of your tan," Kit teased. It was true. Noah's body was a golden color, making the black mat of hair on his chest even more appealing.

He glanced over at her. "You'll get your share today. Come here."

Kit's eyes widened. "Why?"

He held out his hand. "You might as well learn how to guide the *Rainbow*. Come on, don't look so scared. It's easy."

She grimaced. "Next you'll be telling me Tripoli does it."

Noah laughed fully, leaning over and gripping her bare arm, pulling her to her feet. "Come on, my hesitant sailor."

Grudgingly Kit placed her hands on the wheel, her feet slightly apart to compensate for the gentle rolling motion of the vessel. Noah stood behind her, both arms around her as he helped Kit get the feel of the helm. She was agonizingly aware of the warmth of his male body against her, of having nowhere to break contact with him. Her heartbeat rose and she tensed.

"Relax," he said close to her ear. "I don't bite, contrary to popular feminist opinion."

Kit twisted her head, trying to give him a dirty look. "As I've said before, no man is unarmed."

Noah's green eyes danced with laughter, his smile teasing. "As if women don't have their own arsenal," he taunted.

"Such as?" Kit challenged, enjoying their repartee.

He rested his head on her shoulder for a moment, amusement lacing his rich, husky voice. "Such as, 'I've got a headache tonight, Fred' or—"

Kit gave him a jab in the ribs. "You—"

Noah stepped away, laughing. "Don't say it! I know I'm a chauvinist. Let's face it," he said, coming back and standing dangerously close to her again as she gripped the wheel, "if you didn't have me around to tease you a little, you'd get serious about feminism."

Kit gave him a black look, an unwilling grin tugging at the corners of her mouth despite everything she could do to stop it. "You can go, but Tripoli can stay."

He feigned being wounded, coming up and sliding his hands suggestively across her shoulders. "You mean you'd make me walk the plank?"

"Where's the plank?" Kit called in a loud voice.

Noah looked over at the dog. "Tripoli, I think she means it! You're going to have to save me from getting torn apart by the sharks. Quick! Be my life raft!"

Kit laughed in gales, unable to stop. It felt so good to laugh, to let go of that professional barrier that always existed between them while on board the *Osprey*. The last month had altered their relationship subtly, and she relished the new intimacy with him. Finally Noah took the helm, guiding her to the chair so she could sit and giggle. The wind was brisk, and the tangy scent of the ocean was a delicious intoxicant. Occasionally Noah would cast a spurious glance in her direction, one brow crooked at a questioning angle. He guided the boat along the coast, rarely more than a mile offshore. Tripoli lazed at Kit's feet, sleeping.

"Truce?" Noah hedged finally.

"You think you deserve one after those earlier remarks?" Kit demanded.

He shrugged his broad shoulders. "Let's take a democratic vote by the crew." He glanced down at Tripoli. "I'm sure I'll get reinstated that way."

"Let's not and say we did. I don't think there's much democracy aboard this boat of yours."

"I think you're right. Feel like going down to the galley and getting us something cool to drink?"

Kit shrugged indifferently, feigning a yawn. "Sorry, I have a headache."

It was his turn to grin. "Touché. I wish I had a mirror right now."

"Why?"

"To show you just how lovely and relaxed you've become."

Kit groaned, getting to her feet. "I'll be back in a minute."

Opening the doors to the cabin of the boat, Kit stepped carefully down the polished mahogany steps. Bunk beds were built into one wall, the deep golden wood burnished and smooth beneath her fingertips as she made her way toward the tiny galley. Passing the bathroom, Kit spotted a mirror. Out of curiosity, she ventured in and looked at her reflection. The difference was startling! Noah was right—her gray eyes sparkled with happiness, her cheeks were flushed with life and her lips curved upward, free of tension.

Climbing back up to the deck with their refreshments, Kit handed Noah a soft drink and sat down in her chair.

"Thanks," he said, meaning it.

"You're welcome. You really do have a beautiful boat, Noah."

"It's my sanity when things start closing in on me over at the Coast Guard."

Kit understood what he meant—the brutal number of hours and days he'd put in since Morgan had been branded a traitor. "You don't get to do this very often, though, do you?"

"No, maybe three or four times a year." He shared a warm look with her. "But until Garcia is caught, this is now officially your second home."

Kit eyed him speculatively. "Maybe," she hedged. "That's all I need—a boat as a second home."

"You're teaching me to take time out from the job and relax."

There was a difference in Noah, Kit conceded. When she had first met him, he'd been a driven officer who was married to his career for good reasons. But since she'd been living with him, he'd been taking more and more time away from his job. Weekends were spent relaxing whenever possible. They had a positive effect on each other, she decided.

Noah turned, catching her thoughtful gaze. "Besides, I like to fish for our dinner. Saves on grocery bills," he teased.

Kit tried to ignore the fact that he'd said, "our" dinner. She tilted her head. "Tell me, Noah, why aren't you married?"

Noah turned the boat in a westerly direction as they rounded an outcrop of rock, heading toward a small cove ringed with palm trees and a white beach in the distance. "I was planning on a family about five years ago, and then this fiasco with Morgan blew up in our faces. Since then I've had to devote all my spare time to keeping my own career intact from officers who wanted to see me leave the Coast Guard. No one wanted the brother of a traitor in the ranks. So, for a long time I slaved twelve hours a day, seven days a week to salvage my career and ensure that no one could drum me out before I put in the twenty years required for my pension."

"It's not fair that you or Aly should be punished like that," Kit growled unhappily.

"Life is never fair. We just have to learn how to roll with the punches." His eyes crinkled with sudden amusement. "Besides it's only been recently that I've felt like settling down. I had plenty of wild oats to sow."

"I'll bet you did."

"Now there you go again, accusing me."

Kit grimaced. "With your good looks, I'm sure you have an army of women waiting in line to snag you."

"Jealous?"

She clamped her mouth shut, embarrassed by his gentle taunting.

"Let's put it this way. I've had a few serious relationships in the past and I enjoy women. Are you going to hang me for that?"

Kit approved of his honesty. "No. I'm the one who should get hung out to dry for the way I've fouled up my life."

Noah shook his head. "Mistakes are allowed, Kit. It's when you keep making the same mistake that it becomes stupidity." He shared a smile with her. "Ignorance is forgivable. Stupidity isn't."

"For once we agree."

Noah guided the boat into the cove. The blue-green water sparkled a crystal invitation as he slowly approached the sandy white beach. About ten feet offshore, he cut the engine and heaved the anchor overboard. He looked up at her.

"Well, are you ready to go snorkeling with me to catch our picnic lunch?"

She smiled and nodded, following him to the lower deck, where the equipment was stored in a large wooden locker. Kit slid out of her shorts. She felt immediate heat in her cheeks when she noticed Noah watching her with a hungry glimmer in his eyes. Almost immediately he veiled his gaze, and she took a deep, shaky breath in relief.

Noah pulled out several articles from the box. "Okay, here you go. One set of flippers, a face mask and a snorkel." He handed them to her, then retrieved his own set of gear.

The rest of the day was a little slice of heaven for Kit. It started when she eased herself into the warm, welcoming waters of the cove with Noah's steadying hand on her waist. She learned quickly with his instructions, and in no time they were swimming around the cove, watching hundreds of brilliantly colored tropical fish. The entire floor was carpeted with a fortress of coral. Tripoli had leaped off the boat earlier, immediately swimming to shore, happily exploring his new domain. Kit laughed as she saw the Doberman collecting fallen palm fronds on the beach as if they were prize bones.

For more than an hour, she experienced an intense joy with Noah at her side. He speared two sea bass. Afterward they swam to shore to roast them over the open flames of a small fire. Kit sat on a blanket sharing a lunch of fish, cantaloupe and potato salad with Noah. His body gleamed from the recent swim, and she enjoyed the play of muscles each time he moved.

"Sure you aren't a fish?" Kit asked between flaky bites of sea bass.

"Probably am. I was born in Clearwater and learned to swim when I was five years old."

"It's nice to see someone really enjoy himself," Kit said.

Noah sat cross-legged, balancing a cup of wine in one hand and his plate in the other. "I learned early on in this game to keep some distance between drug busting and my personal life, Kit." He looked gratefully around the cove. "This place has been a real haven and heaven to me when the pressure gets rough."

"I believe it," she whispered. Her appetite over the past month had improved markedly, and Kit ate with relish. "I never separated narc work from my home life." And then she added with a grimace, "I really didn't have a home life." Finishing off the meal, Kit put the plate aside and wrapped her hands around her legs to rest her chin on her knees. The cove was alive with color.

"You do now," Noah said. "In all fairness to you, though, doing undercover work is totally different from sea-busting activity. I don't live in the trenches the way you did. If we find one low-profile boat a day, that's usually good hunting for us. You lived with the element, rubbing elbows with the pimps, the junkies and the dealers." He gave her a keen look. "And you paid the price for it, too."

Pleasantly tired, Kit closed her eyes, turning her head in his direction. "Too much for one, looking back on it," she admitted.

Noah repacked the picnic basket, his lips thinning. "Kit, if you had a choice right now, would you quit narc?"

The question startled her. That, plus the carefully concealed strength in his voice. She lifted her lashes to study him. "Want the truth?"

Noah gave her a gentle smile. "Has there ever been anything but that between us?"

Managing a short laugh, Kit stretched out on the blanket before him, luxuriating in the rays of the hot sun. "That's one of our unfailing attributes as a team, I'm afraid."

"I find it an important one," he countered.

Kit eyed him suspiciously, deciding not to ask him why. "That aside, yes, I'd quit narc today if I could."

"Why don't you?"

She frowned. "You read my personnel file. I'm up to my hocks with Garcia and the Colombian connection." She rested her arm against her eyes, muttering, "Chuck needs me on this bust, Noah. I told him it would be the last one. I can't take it anymore."

Noah forced himself to sit quietly at her side, his heart contradicting at the pained admission slipping from her lips. He stared down at her. Kit looked almost ethereal, but he could also see strength and courage in the set of her full, promising lips. Not to mention that telltale flash of silver in her large gray eyes from time to time. He reached over, running his fingers lightly down her arm, and captured her hand briefly, giving it a squeeze.

"What would you do if you quit?"

Kit thrilled to his unexpected touch. As always, Noah had caught her off guard. She removed her arm from across her eyes and looked up into his strong, clean face. The intimacy between them was one of silent, mutual agreement, and it rattled her completely.

"I have a minor in teaching. I'd like to go back to college and get my certificate. Then I'd like to work with kids in the elementary grades."

His green eyes darkened. "You'd be one hell of a teacher." Noah felt himself growing hard with desire and fought to restrain himself. Frustration curdled in his throat. Reluctantly he forced a smile. "Let's rest for an hour and then we'll go for a swim," he suggested, rolling over on his belly and lying next to her.

Kit's lips parted, and she was aware of her rapidly beating heart. The need for Noah filled her. Without another word, she lay on her back and closed her eyes, excruciatingly aware of Noah's body only inches away from her.

Chapter Nine

Come on," Noah coaxed, "let's take one more swim around the cove." He rose and offered his hand to Kit. After an hour's nap, both were refreshed. Kit's gray eyes shone, and as Noah saw desire lingering in their depths, it hit him physically. His strong, bronzed fingers wrapped around her hand and he pulled her gently upward. It would be so easy...so easy to pull her those last few inches that separated them into his arms, lean down and...

"No—" Kit whispered, alarmed as she looked into his hooded eyes and read his intent. Some small part of her fought her desire because it was wrong to entangle their professional relationship with a personal one. But the protest dissolved as she became helplessly ensnared within his sea-green gaze.

Noah maintained a hold on Kit's hand, poignantly aware of her warmth. He saw her eyes grow dark, and felt himself being drawn into a vortex of heat. His grip tightened and he pulled Kit forward until their bodies met and touched like hot, molten steel. He knew he shouldn't, but another part of him, the part that wanted to give her the happiness she had long deserved, won out. He reached out and gently caressed her cheek. Placing his finger beneath her chin, he gently forced her to meet his mouth. The dangerous world they lived in no longer existed. Only Kit and her beautiful gray eyes telling him so much did.

Something old and painful broke loose in Kit's heart as Noah's mouth gently brushed hers. She felt his hands cradle her shoulders, bringing her fully against him. Her breathing grew chaotic as she slid her hands up his arms and across his shoulders.

"Kit..." Noah whispered against her lips, his breath moist, fanning across her cheek. He ran his tongue across her lips, tasting the ocean salt, feeling her quiver. "Yes," he coaxed thickly. "Yes..."

Kit uttered a small cry, melting against his sun-warmed body, her breath stolen from her as Noah deepened his kiss. His mouth was strong, plundering her ripened senses, evoking one major explosion after another throughout her yearning body. She was wildly aware of the hard muscles tensing across his chest, the wiry hair beneath her palm, the clean male scent of him mixed with the sun and the salt tang of the ocean.

His tongue caressed the corners of her lips, inviting her to join him in the exchange that sent a wave of exultation racing through her.

Her breath came in short, shallow gasps as she hungrily returned the questing pressure of his mouth. The world anchored to a halt, the lapping of the waves on the beach heightening the dreamlike cocoon he was weaving around both of them. Noah tasted good. And clean. Her lashes fell softly on the planes of her cheeks, and she slid her arms around him, relinquishing all her disintegrating control to this man who had fanned the fires of her body to life. The experience created a storm of exhilaration, making her crave even more of him.

Noah's hands moved upward from Kit's shoulders to frame her face, and his mouth gloried in her returning passion. Time melted into infinity and Kit leaned heavily against him, caressing the inner softness of her mouth, sending a tumult of wavelike sensations that shuddered deliciously throughout her. Slowly Noah lowered her back to the blanket.

His green eyes were dark, searching hers. Fingers trembling as he caressed her cheek, he whispered, "I need you, Kit."

Wordlessly she nodded. Every nerve in her begged for his continued touch, his fiery onslaught. As his hands moved along the straps of her lavender bathing suit, she sighed deeply, surrendering to him.

Peeling the thin straps from her shoulders, Noah eased the suit off Kit. She was exquisitely perfect—for him. Wanting to worship her, he stood and divested himself of his suit, dropping it to one side.

Kit's heart mushroomed with a suffused glow. She welcomed Noah into her arms as he slid down beside her, and captured her face in his large hand, cradling her chin, forcing her to look up at him. She read so much in those green eyes flecked with depths of gold fire. Kit shivered at the coiled power she felt building explosively around him. She wanted him as much as he wanted her.

Noah outlined her lips with small, hungry kisses. He nibbled at the corner of her mouth and then sent his hot, claiming lips down her slender nape. "You're beautiful," he rasped. "More than beautiful. Perfect..."

A shiver fled through her as his tongue wove wet patterns in the valley between her taut, aching breasts. A moan rose in her throat as he goaded the already hardened nipples into fiery life. Somewhere in the delicious hazy state of her mind, Kit wanted to return the love he was giving her in equal measure. Her hands moved knowingly, down the expanse of his tightly muscled chest, from the flat of his stomach to the rich, carpeted area below. She heard him groan, then felt him tense beside her.

"God, how I want you," Noah gasped, smothering her awaiting lips. He cupped one breast, delighting in its proud, crescent curve, and leaned over to tease it. He felt Kit's nails dig deeply into his shoulders, her body becoming a taut bow against him as he gently tugged on the yielding nipple. Kit tasted good, her perfume and the ocean scent intoxicating to his senses. She felt like firm velvet beneath his exploring hands. His body shrieked for release, but he quelled his own desires in order to bring her pleasure, instead.

Noah rained kisses down the expanse of her stomach, across her slightly rounded abdomen, and gently parted her thighs with his hand. He heard her cry out in fierce need as he tantalized the very core of her being. As he drove her beyond the edge of ecstasy, he realized that she was the most inviting, passionate and willful woman he'd ever met. Her breath was shallow and gasping as he placed his knee between her damp thighs. Her body had a sheen to it and he gently ran his hands upward from her hips and ribs to her beautifully formed breasts and, finally, to her flushed face. Kit's eyes were wide and dazed with fulfillment. He covered her with his male body, moving in accordance with the woven web of desire throbbing heatedly between them. Leaning over, he caressed her full, eager lips and responded to her hungry urgency, glorying in her uninhibited response.

"Now...please now," Kit keened softly. "Please... I need you, Noah..."

He was aware of the boiling heat within him, his own primal animal desire clashing savagely with his control. He eased into her warm depths, dragging in a deep, ragged breath of air. Kit tensed, her fingers clutching his shoulders. She felt like life itself—yielding and fertile to his starving body. Urgency thrummed through him, and all his powerful control exploded in a raging thirst. He thrust deeply, and a growl tore from him.

They were one as they must be, for there was no other way with them. With each matching movement of her responsive body, Noah gloried in their shared joy. He felt Kit tense beneath him and heard a small cry bubble upward from her throat. A look of utter rapture crossed her face, and her lashes lay like sooty fans against her cheeks. He reveled in her climax just as he yielded to his own need to send his seed of life deep within her moments later.

Kit lay gasping against him, spent in the aftermath. "I never knew..." she whispered, moving her hand across Noah's damp chest, giving him a weak embrace.

Noah kissed her temple. "That it could be this good? It can be when it's right," he said thickly, gathering Kit up against him. Their hearts thundered in unison against each other. He kissed her eyelids, her nose and, finally, her wet, full lips.

"You're beautiful, Kitten," he admitted softly.

Kit raised her lashes. A tender light burned deep in his jade-colored eyes and her heart somersaulted with joy. Words were useless. She could feel the depth of his feelings radiating toward her, and she felt humbled by it, swept upward on a rainbow of ecstasy because of it. Loving Noah was without comparison. He made her feel as if the human body were a vessel rendered sacred through their loving act. Kit caressed his cheek, her eyes wide with the wonder of this new discovery.

"You make me feel beautiful."

Noah nodded, understanding. The bond he felt with Kit was almost tangible. He was aware of it with every touch of his hand on her. Tenderly he placed his mouth on her lips, drinking deeply of her. "You've given me so much," he told her, stroking her hair.

Kit shook her head, her voice trembling with emotion. "No, Noah. You've given me a new and better life."

He smiled and rested his cheek against hers, inhaling her sweet scent. "Maybe, maybe not. We've got a lot of tough days ahead of us."

Fear niggled through her as she slid her arms across Noah's shoulders. As she buried her face against his neck, Kit couldn't ignore that seed of terror.

After taking a shower once they arrived home that evening, Kit sat on her bed, worried. Noah's love-making had left her feeling vulnerable and exquisitely feminine. It was as if he had taken away the last of the old Kit Anderson's toughness and bravado forever. Wandering over to the dresser mirror, Kit hesitantly lifted her lashes to stare at herself. She wore a sleeveless light blue blouse and a pair of jeans, but that didn't detract from her as a woman. No, one look into her own eyes and Kit realized how much more had happened. And the future was uncertain. And dangerous. With a sigh Kit opened the door. Regardless of how she felt, dinner had to be made.

In the kitchen she took a checkered apron from one of the drawers and tied it around her waist and began preparing a meal of fried chicken with wild rice. Kit heard a bedroom door open, and then close, and realized Noah was coming.

Turning her head, she saw Noah saunter into the room. He was heartrendingly handsome in the dark blue polo shirt with a pair of khaki shorts, and he gave her a devastating smile of silent welcome. Kit trembled beneath the mesmerizing warmth of his eyes as he walked over to her.

"Can I tell you how happy you look?" Noah whispered as he leaned down and placed a kiss on her lips. It was a long, welcoming kiss meant to convey more than the lightness of his words. Not a second had gone by without Kit in his thoughts. He would never forget the power of their lovemaking. His fingers tightened on her shoulder briefly. "And I'll also make a decidedly male chauvinist comment and tell you how utterly ravishing you look wearing an apron." He dropped another more coaxing kiss. This time he lingered, his mouth barely grazing her warm lips. "Mmm, I think we ought to have dessert before dinner," he teased. He brushed his mouth more strongly against her, delighted by her returning pressure.

Kit gave a low laugh, trying to extricate herself gently from his continued charm. "Noah Trayhern, you're the most enticing man I've ever met, but the answer is no," she murmured, smiling. "Besides, we need to sit down and have a serious talk."

His brows dipped. "Oh?" He caressed the slope of her cheek. Did Kit know how delicious she appeared to him? Her eyes held a special spark of life for the first time, her cheeks were pink from the heat of the kitchen stove, and that smile... He expelled a heavy sigh and tried to be dramatic. Looking down at the assembled animals sitting expectantly at their feet, he addressed them with a twinkle in his eye.

"Okay, gang, what do you think? Is this ravishing woman going to tell me I have to cook dinner, instead?"

Calico meowed sonorously as she got up to rub against Noah's leg.

Kit giggled. "You are the most manipulative person I've ever met! And yes, we're going to talk. And no, I don't mind doing my fair share in the kitchen."

Noah's green eyes darkened with a mischievous glint. He grabbed Kit and imprisoned her seductively against his body. "Okay, would you agree to live here forever and ever if I continue to help you with all the kitchen chores?"

Kit eyed him speculatively. The strength and hardness of his male body sent new waves of surging, hungry awareness through her, and she craved his closeness and his wonderful ability to love her. "Let me go, Noah, before I lose my train of thought!"

She was magical, Noah decided, still bound up in the desire of their explosive lovemaking on the beach. But that was another world, a world of dreams, not reality. And looking into Kit's worried eyes, he felt some of his euphoria begin to evaporate. Releasing her, he went to the refrigerator and pulled out a bottle of chilled white wine. "I think this is going to call for a drink," he murmured, taking down two glasses and setting them on the table.

The mood altered, and Kit lost her smile. "This isn't going to be easy, Noah."

He matched her seriousness, pouring wine into one of the glasses, then handing it to Kit. "Okay, honey, what is it?"

Just the tenor of his voice sent a shiver of renewed longing through her. Kit expelled a long breath before beginning.

"This afternoon—"

Noah reached across the table, his hand covering hers. "It was special, Kit. For both of us."

She moistened her lips, raising her eyes to meet his honest gaze. "Yes. Yes, it was, Noah. And more than anything, I want to be honest with you." She swallowed hard, removing her hand. "In my job as an undercover agent I lied all the time, Noah. I lied to stay alive. I've got five years of lying under my belt. Worst of all, I find it easy to lie to myself more than anyone. When I'm scared on a narc job, I lie to myself and pretend I don't feel the fear. And when I was at an emotional breaking point I used to stick my head in the sand by working harder, hoping to forget it." Kit took a fortifying sip of the wine to shore up her raw emotional state. One look at Noah's open face gave her the courage to go on. "So that brings it around to us."

"Go on," Noah said softly.

Kit closed her eyes. "This afternoon was the most beautiful experience in my life, Noah. It was one positive against so much negativity I've lived with for five years. But—'' She chewed on her lower lip for a second. "This is so hard," Kit confessed, seeking his silent assurance.

Noah grimaced. "Just say it, Kit. Let your feelings speak. We can handle it."

Kit shook her head. "You're always so positive."

"Do you like the alternative?" Noah probed.

"No. Okay, the bottom line is . . . until this thing is settled with Garcia, I can't sleep with you, Noah."

He sat back, digesting her comment. At that moment Kit was searching and unsure. He offered her a slight smile meant to reinforce her honesty. "You're right. For both of us. It won't be a problem."

Her eyes widened slightly. "No?"

Kit's tensed shoulders fell and she took a deep breath. "I thought you would be angry, Noah. Hurt, maybe—I don't know." She gave him a soulful look of utter relief.

Leaning his elbows on the table, Noah said, "Let's talk about your decision to stay in your bed and out of my arms."

Kit was caught off guard by his concern and calm reaction to her ultimatum. She found it easy to respond. "We're in a terrible predicament with Garcia, complicated by this contract out on my head. We both need to remain clearheaded about our priorities until Operation Storm is over." She stared down at his hands around the wineglass. They were so strong, so loving. "I haven't been with a man for two years. And when I met you, I had no intention of—of—well, going to bed with you.''

"It just kind of happened," Noah admitted quietly. "When I first saw you, I wondered why you dressed in oversize baggy clothes to hide that beautiful, skinny body of yours. Then I realized it was to conceal your obvious femininity. Working in the trenches had made you wary of men in general."

Kit blushed. "You're right. After years of protecting myself from the male criminals I had to live with, you walked into my life and made me feel like a woman again."

Noah's eyes grew warm as he studied her. "You've always been a woman. We just seem to bring out the best in each other."

"I've never before felt the things you've brought out in me. And I mean more than just in bed," Kit hastily added.

"That's a wonderful compliment. Thank you."

She shot him a knowing look. "I have the distinct feeling that everything you touch is in some way better for the experience."

Noah laughed, pouring them both more wine. "You're no slouch, either, Anderson. My life hasn't been the same since you arrived." And then he added, "It's been better. And you're right. We both need to keep our focus on our job and place our personal needs aside for now."

"Yes," Kit agreed. She wanted to tell him that being in his arms was heaven. It was healing and wonderful and... She gave him a tender smile. "You've given me so much in such a short time, Noah. And all of it has been so—'' Kit groped for the words to convey her feelings. ''I don't know how to say it. Only that you've made me feel again. And feel good about myself for the first time in years.'' She reached out, shyly touching his hand, aware of the wiry texture of hair that covered its broad expanse. ''You've given me so much in precious little time, and I want and need time to assimilate it all. To adjust to this new me.'' Kit's eyes grew cautious. ''Our future is like a box of explosives that could detonate in our face at a moment's notice until we collar Garcia. I don't know where we're going with each other, Noah. I only know that we're both worth too much to throw this away on a whim. I need time to iron myself out emotionally. In all fairness to you, I don't feel I've contributed much to our unique arrangement beyond being a moody house guest.''

A smile curved the corners of his mouth. ''If you're talking about getting up and pacing the halls at night, don't give it a second thought.''

She withdrew her hand from his. ''The nightmares have finally stopped. Ever since you held me when I cried, I've been able to sleep nights.''

''Listen to me, Kitten,'' Noah coaxed huskily, ''you're made of silk. You're tough, resilient, beautiful and exotic. Right now you don't know it, but you're one of a kind. I saw that right away in you, and you're in the process of realizing it yourself.''

Tears marred her vision, and Noah's face blurred as Kit looked at him. ''In the time I've been here with you, I have changed for the better. With your help, I've gotten rid of a lot of my past."

"You're on the road to recovery," Noah agreed. And if he was willing to admit it, he thought, he wanted to be a continued part of Kit's healing process. She brought out the best in him.

Kit got to her feet and went to the drain board, staring out the window for a long moment. Finally she turned and leaned against the counter, meeting Noah's patient gaze.

"I'm glad we could talk this out. I feel better."

Noah wanted to go to her and hold her, but it was impossible. He had given his word to back off and wait. Trying to ignore the sensual tension strung tautly between them was going to be tough. The phone rang, breaking that tenuous cord that bound them.

Noah rose and answered the call on the kitchen phone. "Lieutenant Trayhern speaking."

"Trayhern, this is Cordeman."

Flicking a glance over at Kit, Noah found himself automatically wanting to protect her from any more narc activity. His voice hardened. "It's Saturday evening, Cordeman."

"Can't help it. How's our house guest getting along?"

Angry because the police supervisor had interrupted the tenderness he and Kit had shared, Noah growled, "Just fine. What's going on that I deserve the honor of this phone call on the weekend?"

"Just wanted to let you know that the U.S. Navy is picking up an awful lot of activity at all the major choke points. Also, our DEA undercover agent had brought back word that Garcia is getting ready to move the *Marie-Elise*, his personal two-hundred-foot yacht, out for a meeting with smaller drug dealers' boats.''

His hand tightened on the phone, his eyes never leaving Kit's face. "When?"

"No sure answer to that, Lieutenant. All we know is that Garcia is behind the increased drug trafficking you've been meeting head-on the past few weeks. We think he's going to continue this onslaught to try to keep the attention of the CG cutters—clearing the way for him to drop his bales of marijuana in some safe harbor without the possibility of a bust."

"So the pond's heating up." That meant sixteen-hour days and probably weekend duty.

"You got it. The U.S. Navy P3 will be doing a flyover of the Colombian coast to keep an eye on Garcia's ship. When it moves, we know he's going to meet with the dealers. You'll be notified as soon as possible so you and the *Osprey* can get into position."

"Fine," Noah answered.

"Tell your house guest hello for me, will you?"

"Yes." The word came out clipped, and Noah hung up the phone, glaring down at the tiled floor.

Kit moved over to where he stood. "That was Chuck. What did he want?"

Grudgingly Noah filled her in and he saw some of the old terror coming back to Kit's eyes. Unthinkingly he reached out, placing his hand on her shoulder. Damn! Reluctantly he removed his hand. "It's going to be hard not being intimate with you," he muttered, a sour smile on his mouth.

"I know," Kit whispered, moving to a safer distance from Noah. Struggling to maintain a professional demeanor with him, Kit changed subjects. "So Garcia's going to step up the pace of boats smuggling drugs to our coast."

"Yes. He's trying to pull a decoy maneuver so his drop of bales to the dealers will go unimpeded."

Kit turned to face the counter. Their dinner needed to be finished, although in all honesty, she was no longer hungry. She went through the motions of preparing a salad. Noah moved around the room, tightly wound with energy. It felt as if he were going to explode any second.

"Did Chuck say how he's doing?" she asked, wanting to defuse Noah's tension.

Shrugging, Noah sat down, staring moodily at the glass of wine. "Fine, I guess."

"You don't like him, do you?"

"I don't exactly see your old boss as a nice person, no."

She peeled a carrot, slicing it into the bowl. "Why?"

"Cordeman's more concerned with results than he is with his people."

"Isn't that a bit cruel?" Kit demanded, taking issue with his abrupt assessment.

"He used you, Kit. I don't respect someone who burns out his best people."

Kit rested her hands on the sink, feeling she had to defend Chuck. "Look, no one's perfect, Noah. Chuck has his shortcomings, but I'll never forget that he was the only one there for me when the chips were down. He's gruff, yes, but he's not really callous." She chewed on her lower lip, watching Noah's face darken.

His mouth thinned. "Let's not fight, Kit. Particularly over Cordeman. It isn't necessary."

She began to slice a ripe, red tomato. "Okay," she whispered. "Life's too short to spend it on disagreements. God knows, we do enough fighting with the druggies."

"Our home is a haven against that."

She raised her eyes. "That's an understatement. It's the only place where we can escape."

The noose was closing around them. Noah sensed it. "Well, as long as Dante doesn't discover where you are, that's a big point in our favor," he groused, more to himself than her.

She put the tomatoes in the salad, choosing a scallion to add to it. "Every month I lived at Garcia's fortress with Dante at his side, I sweated. I knew the longer I stayed, the higher my chances were of being discovered."

"No wonder you ended up with stomach ulcers."

Kit pursed her lips. "Well, Chuck told me ulcers and migraines are the occupational hazards of an undercover agent."

"So much for Cordeman's philosophy. If he'd taken better care of you, the ulcers wouldn't have been the outcome."

Kit ignored the jab, realizing that no matter what she said about her other boss, Noah wasn't going to agree. A shiver coursed down her spine.

"What's wrong?"

"Nothing," Kit muttered, wiping her hands on a towel.

Noah got to his feet, placing his hands on her shoulders and turning her to face him. God, she looked incredibly unguarded at that moment. He couldn't stop himself from reaching out and caressing her flushed cheek. "Tell me," he commanded.

Kit shivered beneath Noah's low, disturbing voice. She took an unsteady breath, aware of the desire within her to kiss that male mouth that tore her senses apart. He lifted her above every fear and depression into the yearning euphoria she hungered to explore with him again. She saw so much in his eyes, wanting to lose herself within them and know that she was safe. A broken smile came to her lips.

"It's Dante," she admitted.

He searched Kit's very still face, and his hands tightened on her shoulders. "And?"

"Dante's a snake, Noah." Her eyes glazed with the remembrance that had haunted her nightly dreams with regularity. "I worked with that sick bastard for a year down there at the Colombian fortress. I sweated around Dante more than all of them put together. I never knew if he was going to pull a knife on me or what."

"Did he try to—"

She grimaced. "No, thank God. He had other preferences besides women. I suppose I should be thankful, but..." Her voice trailed off as she relived one frightening episode with Dante. She felt Noah's hand sliding down her hair in a reassuring gesture. Forcing a smile, Kit said, "I'm too old for this business, Noah. I've seen too much."

"Maybe you ought to resign," he murmured, "and go after that teaching certificate."

Reluctantly Kit withdrew from him, turning to put the salad on the table. "Maybe I should."

Frustrated by the vise Kit was caught in, Noah busied himself setting the table. He wanted to say; *Dammit, Cordeman has pulled out every human emotion you had and then put it through a blender, Kit. You need a nice safe job like teaching. You don't need street action to tear holes in your stomach and shatter your senses.* But he remained silent, realizing Kit would no more quit Operation Storm than Cordeman would. Was her life worth getting Garcia? He didn't think so, wishing mightily for an escape for her. But there was none. They had to take things one week at a time, netting the drug dealers trying to reach the Florida coast, waiting and watching for Garcia to make his move.

Chapter Ten

Something was wrong. Kit could sense it. After another grueling month of seven-day weeks, she had come down with stomach flu on Friday and stayed home. Noah had left that morning without her for the first time. She glanced at the clock on the kitchen wall: it was now 8:00 p.m. He'd promised that if he was going to be late, someone from Coast Guard headquarters would notify her. But no call had come. Where was he?

The police portion of her brain began to work overtime. Dante and his contract killers were making every effort to find her, according to the snitches. Had they discovered that Noah was protecting her? Had they kidnapped him as he stepped off the *Osprey*?

Killed him? She escaped to the living room, a deep sense of anguish searing through her.

Biting her lower lip, Kit stared at the front door. *Come through the door,* she begged silently. *Please, Noah, just come home....* Burying her face in her hands, Kit forced herself to take a deep breath. What was happening to her? Living with Noah since they had made love had been like a never-ending dream. The warmth between them was undeniable, just as the longing in his stormy green eyes when she caught him staring at her during quiet moments at home was nearly unbearable. They wanted each other so badly. But if they allowed their emotions to rule their heads, it would take their alertness away from the danger that surrounded them, and possibly get them killed.

Kit paced back and forth from the living room to the foyer. She had planned a special dinner for Noah tonight to let him know how much she missed being at his side. Her lips thinned, and she walked over to the phone sitting on the lamp table in the living room. She had to call someone... but whom? She picked up the address book on the table and flipped to the last page where Noah had scribbled the number he could be reached at in an emergency.

Her hand hovered over the phone. She wasn't supposed to make a call for any reason! The line might be tapped, and her cover would be blown. Snitches who worked for Dante could be anywhere. Kit's eyes narrowed as she stared down at the phone. Swallowing convulsively, she made the decision. Just as she touched the receiver, the phone rang. Startled, Kit jerked her hand back, her heart slamming against her rib cage.

The phone rang four times before she reached out to pick up the receiver. She wasn't supposed to answer the phone either, but Kit couldn't combat the terror she was experiencing....

"We've got a live one, Skipper," Joe said excitedly.

Handing the hot list to the ensign, Noah smiled grimly. "The *Sanchez* is registered in the U.S. This is our lucky day."

Noah motioned for the ensign to take over the helm, and watched the hundred-foot ship bobbing a mile away from them. "This is the second one today," he muttered, thinking that this meant he wasn't going to make it home before midnight. The sun had already set. Worried about Kit all day, he hadn't been as alert as he might have been. She had been deathly sick all night. This morning when he'd gone to her bedroom, she'd still been weak from the flu.

"She's definitely low profile," Joe said, pointing at the ship.

"Yes." Twisting around, Noah ordered the boarding party to prepare for another search.

The *Osprey* came alive, but Noah remained seemingly immune to the sudden activity surrounding him. The thrumming of the *Osprey*'s mighty engines accelerating to close the distance between it and the *Sanchez* filled the air. He pulled his baseball cap an inch lower, his gaze intent on the other boat.

"You taking this boarding, Skipper?" Edwards wanted to know.

"Yes. I'll run it from the deck of the *Sanchez*. You stay on the bridge and coordinate the radio and other necessary communications."

Edwards's blue eyes danced with excitement. "I wish it was my turn."

A thread of a noncommittal smile pulled at Noah's mouth. He was aware of everything at the moment. Adrenaline was surging through his bloodstream, heightening his five senses and giving him that extra-sensory perception that might be needed—might save him or one of his men from death by a smuggler's bullet. "Next time, Joe," he murmured.

Noah took the binoculars and watched the activity aboard the *Sanchez*. The ship listed and wallowed like a pregnant whale, far below the safety waterline. Noah counted three open hatches on her deck. Scowling, he put down the binoculars.

"I've got a bad feeling about this one, Joe."

The ensign nodded, skillfully easing the *Osprey* alongside the *Sanchez*. "Three hatches. Not good. The hold must be huge. They could have gunmen hiding down there anywhere." Edwards passed a quick look to his skipper. "Just be careful..."

Noah was handed an M-16 rifle by a member of the boarding party. A slight grin touched his mouth. "I've got everything in the world to live for, Joe. I'm not about to waste my life on a drug runner." He placed the portable radio on his belt and stepped from the bridge. "I'll stay in touch once we get aboard," he promised.

Vaguely Noah heard Edwards's commanding voice coming over the PA system, ordering the *Sanchez* to heave to and allow them to board. Noah's mind was on his work, but his heart lingered on Kit. It was true. He did have everything to live for. He'd found Kit. Noah walked down the immaculate deck of the *Osprey* to join his waiting five-man party. Like the crew, Noah was dressed in the one-piece dark blue Coast Guard uniform. They all wore flak jackets.

Petty Officer Jack Formen approached him. "We're ready, Skipper."

"Good. Lock and load," Noah ordered his men quietly. The metallic sound of ammunition magazines being loaded into the lethal weapons was heard. The *Osprey* loomed over the *Sanchez*. Noah saw only two half-naked crewmen in sight. They were dark skinned. Probably Colombian. His jaw clenched as his gaze swept across the vessel. His instincts told him the rest of the motley crew was down in the hold, waiting.

"What do you think?" Noah asked Formen.

The petty officer of forty-five shook his graying head. "Not good, Skipper. This tub's too big to be run by those two dudes."

Noah's mouth quirked as he nodded, bracing himself to compensate for the movement of the *Osprey*. "Yeah...okay, men, let's watch ourselves very carefully," he warned the party.

Noah gave Formen a nod, and the six men leaped from one ship deck to the other. The three hatches looked like yawning, cavernous mouths to Noah. He ordered McMorrison, the youngest crewman, to detain and search the two *Sanchez* men standing on the bridge. Noah's sensitive nostrils detected the sweet odor of marijuana. He motioned Formen to his side.

"You take the first hatch."

"Yes, sir."

Noah looked at the other two men. "Dawson and Crinita, you take the second hatch. I'll take the third."

"Yes, sir," Dawson said.

Noah turned to the last man, Sullivan. "You wait up here in case we get into trouble," he commanded.

"Yes, sir."

The silence became deafening as Noah walked lightly across the cluttered deck laden with coils of rope. The *Sanchez* was a garbage scow, with rust in evidence everywhere. In the gray light of dusk, everything became indistinguishable. They would have to descend those wooden ladders into either total darkness or dimly lit areas where precious seconds would be lost until their eyes adjusted.

Noah's heart began a slow pound as he released the M-16's safety, readying the weapon. His hand tightened around the rifle and he slowed his step, trying to discern if anyone was waiting with gun in hand at the bottom of the hold. His eyes couldn't pierce the gloom. Noah walked cautiously around the hold, lifting his head momentarily to see if Formen or the other team had descended yet. They were getting ready to go down. Sweat trickled down his temples. Gripping the splintered ladder and swinging over the hold entrance, he winced at the powerful odor of marijuana. Grimly Noah glanced around. The feeble light from several electric light bulbs left huge areas of gray shadow throughout the cavernous hold.

Noah descended to the lower deck, turning, his back against the ladder. Silence. He pulled the radio from his belt. Putting his mouth close to it, he pressed the button. "Nothing so far, Joe. Stay alert," he ordered.

Replacing the radio, Noah allowed his hearing to do the work for him. His eyes were adjusting and he saw his other three men coming down into the hold. Bales of tightly wrapped and freshly dried marijuana were packed everywhere with the exception of a few key aisles.

There was the sound of a metallic click. Cold horror washed over Noah. "Formen!" he yelled, "look out!" and assumed a crouched position.

Before Formen could react, the roar of gunfire shattered the silence. The petty officer was knocked off his feet. He slumped to the deck, wounded. The smell of spent ammunition stung Noah's flared nostrils as he raced down the central aisle toward his wounded crewman. Screams, curses and more gunfire mingled in earsplitting explosions all around him. Noah saw four *Sanchez* crewmen hiding behind bales, firing away at his men. Everything blanked out in his mind except the imperative to pin down the enemy.

"Crinita, Dawson!" he roared, "four men at eleven o'clock!" He threw himself flat on the hard surface of the deck, rolling over twice as his men fired in that direction. Finding protection against a bale, Noah glanced toward Formen, who lay unconscious only twenty feet away. Blood was pooling rapidly to surround the area where he lay. The bluish haze of gunfire drifted through the poorly lit hold, the vicious red-and-yellow flames from the muzzles of the rifles ripping through the air.

Sweat covered Noah's face as he gestured for Dawson and Crinita to outflank the *Sanchez* crewmen. Grabbing his radio, Noah shouted orders back to Edwards.

"We need help! Get a medic over here. Formen's down!" Dammit, Formen was bleeding to death! Noah shouldered the M-16, aiming carefully, firing. Dawson and Crinita were working their way into position to pin down the enemy. If only... Noah flipped the rifle on full automatic, spraying at the *Sanchez* crewmen. He lurched to his feet, laying down a blistering wall of fire that gave him cover as he sprinted to where Formen lay.

Noah looked up as he stood over his petty officer. Sullivan was waiting anxiously at the top of the hold.

"Get ready to take him up!" Noah yelled. "I'll push him up the ladder!"

Dropping his weapon, Noah pulled Formen into his arms. He had to get him topside or he would die! Grunting from the weight, Noah maneuvered Formen to the ladder and pushed him upward. Helping hands reached downward, hooking beneath For-men's armpits. With one mighty shove, Noah boosted the unconscious petty officer up and out of the hold to safety. Another spate of gunfire erupted. Wood splintered and exploded all around him. Noah clenched his teeth, dropping to the deck below. In those horrifying seconds, he knew he was the target they were gunning for. Suddenly life became precious as Noah leaned down to grab his rifle. But a bullet found him and he was slammed to the deck. He felt a searing flame of white heat in his left arm as an electric jolt ripped up into his shoulder and neck.

He shook his head to clear the shock of being hit and hung on to his weapon with his right hand. A *Sanchez* crewman suddenly leaped from behind a bale and ran toward him, his revolver lifted. As Noah tried to raise his left arm to steady the wavering barrel of his rifle, he found he couldn't move his fingers.

The crewman sprinted closer, screaming curses. He waved the revolver wildly in his right hand and bore down on Noah, who stood between him and freedom via the hold ladder. Noah gasped as he forced his left arm to move. He had to lift the rifle or he'd be dead in seconds. Blood flowed heavily from his arm, stain-ing his uniform, as he forced his numbed left fingers to steady the weapon.

The crewman was lowering the revolver. Aiming it directly at Noah's chest as he leaped the last few feet toward the ladder. Noah heard Dawson scream at the crewman to drop the gun. He didn't. Noah lifted the M-16. Pain raged through the left side of his body as he squeezed the trigger. The jerk of the rifle tore through him and he cried out, dropping the weapon after firing it, rolling onto his side and grabbing his left shoulder. The *Sanchez* crewman was hurled backward by the impact of the bullet, dead.

"Son of a bitch," Noah sobbed between clenched teeth. Blood. He was bleeding heavily. His mind was clearing, but he knew he was in shock. One look at his forearm and he knew the bullet had severed a major artery. He would bleed to death right here. *No!* his heart screamed. *Kit. What about Kit? Dammit, you can't bleed to death!* He was aware of Dawson running down the aisle, kneeling at his side.

"Get me a tourniquet," Noah gasped. "Anything . . . for God's sake, hurry!"

Dawson's eyes widened as he stared down at his skipper. "Yes, sir!" he breathed, scrambling up the ladder and yelling for the corpsman.

Noah fell back, pressing as hard as he could on the injured area. Closing his eyes, he fought off the first tidal wave of blackness. *I don't want to die in this lousy hold. I want to live. Kit . . . Dammit, I want to live! Got to have time for Kit . . . Isn't the bleeding going to stop?* Noah groaned as he felt his strength begin to ebb. He'd lost too much blood and his eyesight was dimming. If he lost consciousness, his hand would slip from the wound. Where was help? Where the hell was Dawson with a tourniquet? And Jack . . . Jack Formen. God, was he still alive? *Kit . . . I need you . . .* Anger mingled with despair and Noah felt coldness seeping into his lower extremities. He knew what that meant. He lay sprawled on the splintered wooden deck between huge bales of marijuana, wondering if he was going to die without being able to tell Kit just how much she meant to him....

Kit wrapped her hand around the receiver shakily, then finally jerked it off the cradle. "Hello," she croaked, trying to steady her voice.

"Kit, this is Cordeman."

Her knuckles whitened as she tightened her grip on the receiver. "What's wrong, Chuck?" she gasped.

"There was a firefight involving the *Osprey*. Trayhern and another Coast Guard crewman were wounded in the action. They're being brought to the trauma unit of the naval hospital in Miami."

No! her heart screamed. The trauma unit was reserved for critical cases only. Noah had been involved in a gun incident. "Oh, my God," she cried.

"They'll be arriving shortly by Coast Guard helicopter. There's an emergency team standing by and—"

Kit dropped the phone and raced to her bedroom to grab her purse. She didn't care if she blew her cover by showing up in a public place. Noah was injured and she wasn't going to wait patiently at home for further word on him. She took the keys to the silver Toyota, which Noah used as a second car. Using the automatic garage door opener, Kit waited impatiently for the door to lift. *Hurry! Hurry!* Her world was suddenly blown apart. Noah, loving, trusting Noah, who always smiled and looked on the positive side of life, had been shot. How bad was it? What kind of gun? Depending on the type, the bullet could do minimal or maximum damage. She swallowed against the lump in her throat as she backed the Toyota out of the driveway, intent on only one thing: being with Noah.

Kit tore through the trauma unit, almost colliding with Chuck Cordeman as he stood outside the double doors to the restricted area where the critically injured were treated.

Cordeman's eyes narrowed. "Kit? What the hell are you—"

Anxiously she looked around. "Noah. Where is he, Chuck?" she demanded breathlessly.

Cordeman jerked a thumb toward the doors. "In there."

Kit started to push by him, but he grabbed her arm and pulled her back.

"Have you lost your mind?" he demanded. "What the hell's gotten into you? You're supposed to stay out of sight!"

Kit was sobbing breathlessly. She had run all the way from the parking lot after hearing more details on the radio about the gun battle at sea. "Let me go, Chuck." She turned, fully intending to go through those doors with or without Cordeman's consent.

"You're outa your mind!" Cordeman snarled. "Trayhern's the least wounded. Just a bullet through his left arm. They're prepping him for surgery right now. There's nothing you can do—"

Kit glared at him. "Like hell there isn't!" Wresting her arm from his hand, she pushed through the doors. Adrenaline poured through her bloodstream, heightening her senses to an incredible degree. In one sweep of the room she spotted a doctor and two nurses working feverishly over a man in a dark blue Coast Guard uniform. Kit immediately walked across the room before an orderly could accost her. She saw Noah's pale face, the pain pulling at his mouth. Tears jammed into her eyes once more. As she stepped up to the gurney, Noah's eyes widened slightly.

"Kit..." he rasped thickly.

"I'm sorry," the blond nurse said, turning to Kit, "you're going to have to leave."

"Let her stay," Noah begged weakly to the doctor on his left.

The physician hesitated, took one look at Kit and decided to let her remain. "You can only stay for a minute or so. We've just given him a shot and we're taking him to surgery. He'll be unconscious shortly."

Nodding, Kit swallowed hard. She slipped by the nurse and into the cramped cubicle. Tears slid down her cheeks as she surveyed Noah. Blood was splattered all over the front of his uniform; his left forearm was wrapped in a blood-soaked bandage, indicating the area of the wound. A pint of plasma hung from the IV unit above his head, and the needle was inserted in his right arm.

"Oh, Noah..." she whispered, leaning over, placing her trembling hand on his forehead. His brow was damp with perspiration and she saw the ravages of pain lingering in his dark green eyes. He stared confusedly up at her.

"You came . . ."

"You knew I would." Anxiously Kit searched his drawn features. "God, I was so worried, Noah—"

"So was I," he whispered, closing his eyes momentarily. He reopened them, gazing darkly up at her. "It was bad. Jack Formen's really hurt, Kit. I don't want to lose him." His mouth thinned with pain. "I've got to talk to Wanda, Formen's wife. I've got to tell her how he is . . ."

"Hush, darling," she murmured, running her hand gently across his hair. "You've been wounded. They're taking you to surgery soon."

Noah shook his head, becoming groggy from the effects of the drug. "No, Kit, I've got to tell his wife . . . God, they love each other so much—" His voice cracked and he closed his eyes.

Kit reached out, gripping his good hand. "I'll talk to her, Noah. I'll tell her. Go to sleep, darling. When you wake up, you'll feel better." She felt the fingers clutch weakly at her hand, and watched helplessly as grief and pain furrowed his brow.

"Kit?" he mumbled, his voice slurring now.

"Right here."

"Kit, I need you. Out there today, when the gunfire started, all I could think of was you. . . ."

She fought back a sob, leaning over the gurney, placing her mouth against his lips. His flesh was cool beneath hers as she pressed a kiss on them. "I'll be here, Noah. Stop fighting the drug. Everything will be taken care of, I promise you."

Kit stared dully at Chuck across the Surgery floor's visitor's lounge. He gave her a disgruntled look in return. Already two hours had passed since they had wheeled Noah into the operating theater. Wanda Formen sat opposite in another plastic lounge chair, waiting in silent anguish, her face drawn. Kit had consoled her earlier as well as she could. With a sigh she rested her elbows on her thighs. She felt like a quagmire of emotions. Noah's last statement had shaken her almost as badly as finding out that he'd been wounded in a gun battle. As they'd wheeled him away and the nurse had guided her toward the elevator, Kit had fought back the tears. And on the way up, Chuck Cordeman had glared at her obvious lack of control of the situation.

He rose ponderously now and walked over to where she sat.

"Mind if I join you?"

Kit shrugged. "If you're going to discuss my being here, you can save your breath."

Cordeman sank heavily into the chair beside her. He stared at her for a long moment before speaking. "You've changed, Kit."

She roused herself with effort. "Maybe I have."

He frowned. "Yeah. It's not like you to blow your cover over something stupid like this."

Kit sucked in a sharp breath, rounding on him. "*Something like this* just happens to be Noah!" she whispered angrily. "He's not some damn statistic, Chuck!"

"You're touchier than a—"

"Go to hell."

"What's gotten into you, Kit? Does this guy mean something to you? I know you've been living under his roof for quite a while. The way you're behaving, I'd think you'd fallen in love with him."

She had to get a grip on herself. "I know this is hard for you to grasp, Chuck, but Noah has helped me more in the past few months than any human being I've encountered in the past five years. Does that make sense? He helped pull me out of a year-long depression, and he fought to get me time off to rest." She glared at him. "Which is something you never did."

Cordeman's mouth turned sour. "Okay, okay. I had that one coming," he growled. "So he's a nice guy in our rotten little business."

Kit wrung her hands, allowing her head to fall forward. She stared blankly down at the polished black-and-white tiles beneath her feet. "He's a better man than either of us has ever had the privilege of knowing," she gritted out. "Or are ever likely to meet in our business."

Chuck snorted. "Enough of the hearts and flowers, Anderson. If you've got an ounce of sense left, you'll get your rear out of here before you're recognized."

"I'm staying," she hissed between clenched teeth, "until hell freezes over, Chuck. And I don't care if you don't like it. You're not my boss anymore."

Kit rose and began to pace the length of the corridor. Her heart was lost in a cauldron of emotions. The gun battle had ripped away all pretense of how she really felt toward Noah. Halting, Kit closed her eyes, her hand pressed to her chest because it hurt so much. She loved Noah.

A trembling sigh broke from her as she allowed the realization to sink it. When had it happened? How? Just living with Noah had dissolved those wary walls around her heart.

The look in his dark, agony-filled eyes had told her she meant much more than she'd dared admit to him, too. They'd both been fighting to ignore what they really felt. Raising her head, Kit knew what must be done: Noah couldn't know that she loved him. Not until Operation Storm was completed. It would be too hard on both of them.

And did Noah love her? She knew that what she felt was love. A love that had gently captured her and would never let her go. Noah had shown her that real, caring people existed. Did he love her, or was his attention and care merely that, and born of his proximity to her the past months? Uncertain, Kit shuffled slowly back down the hall. Nearly losing Noah had torn away any self-deception she'd cloaked their relationship in. And the future held nothing but more danger. Her love was going to be brutally tested.

A surgical nurse was the first to leave the operating room, and she headed in Kit's direction.

"Ms. Anderson?"

Kit anchored herself to the spot, her heart thrashing in her breast. "Yes?"

She smiled tiredly, taking off the face mask. "Lieutenant Trayhern is going to be fine. We're putting him in recovery and it should be about an hour before he's conscious."

Relief flooded Kit and she closed her eyes. "When may I see him?" Her voice sounded faint to her ears.

"Just as soon as he's conscious and in his private room."

"Thank you," Kit whispered, reaching out and touching the nurse's shoulder. She turned away so that Cordeman couldn't see her face or the tears that dribbled down her cheeks.

Noah groaned, the sound reverberating like a kettle drum through his head. Dizziness was interwoven with nausea as he fought to surface from the powerful anesthetic. His mind was shorting out, with blips of the gun battle, Kit's anxious face and the hammering recoil of an M-16 combining to rip through his semiconscious state. His whole being centered on Kit. He loved her, dammit! And he was bleeding to death in a dark hold. Was he going to slip over the edge to oblivion without ever having told her how damn much he loved her?

Kit, I need you! I don't want to die! You have to know—

"Noah," Kit soothed, leaning over the bed, caressing his sweaty brow, "it's all right. You're safe and you're going to live."

Noah concentrated on Kit's unsteady voice. His eyes felt weighted, and it took every last vestige of strength to force them open. Kit's face danced out of focus before him. He felt the warmth of her breath against his face as she pressed her lips to his. Did she know how good she felt to him?

"You're here," he rasped thickly. "I'm alive..."

Kit cradled his bristly cheek with her hand. "You almost bled to death, Noah. But the doctors fixed the artery." Tears welled up in her eyes.

He saw her tears, a broken smile pulling at his mouth. "Just a close call. God, I'm glad you're here. I kept thinking I'd never get to see you again."

She traced his wrinkled brow with her fingertips. "Welcome back," she whispered.

Exhaustion lapped at Noah. Even now, he knew that with his wound, it would probably be at least six to eight weeks before they'd allow him to skipper the *Osprey* once again. And during that time, Kit would be going out to sea every day without him. Sliding into unconsciousness, he felt his joy over living snuffed out by nightmares. Kit would be out on the pond, a possible target herself. The world was closing in on them like a noose around their necks.

Chapter Eleven

Kit boarded the *Osprey* as she had for the past three months. The only difference was, this time Noah was at her side again, completely recovered from his gunshot wound. She traded greetings with the crew as they walked across the plank and went to the bridge.

Kit stood aside as Joe Edwards thrust out his hand to Noah. "Good to see you back, Skipper. The *Osprey* is all yours."

Noah smiled and shook Joe's proffered hand. "Thank you. You took good care of her in my absence."

A grin spread across Joe's affable face. "I took good care of both your ladies while you were shore-bound, Skipper."

Laughing, Noah agreed.

"How you feeling today, Kit?" Joe inquired.

She mustered a proper grimace. It was always the first question asked, because there wasn't a day that went by that she didn't become seasick. "The usual, Joe."

"You'd think that in time you'd adjust to this," Edwards jibed good-naturedly, trading a look with his skipper.

Noah gave a soft snort, stowing the navigation charts beneath the console. "She's the first person I've ever met who's never adjusted to sea life."

"Just proves I'm not a mermaid, Noah Trayhern," Kit reminded him tartly, making herself comfortable on one of the bridge chairs.

Noah gave her a wicked look in return, one filled with longing. How had three months since he'd been wounded pass so quickly? Noah drank in her fragile form. Kit had never regained the weight she should have, due to her constant seasickness.

Sipping the coffee that the second mate had given her, Kit watched Noah pilot the *Osprey* out of the berth and into the channel. His eyes were narrowed in concentration, his sensitive hands gripping the helm, monitoring every slight change in the ship's course. Hands she now longed to have love her again.... Kit closed her eyes, savoring the ache in her heart. Their home life had changed, their affection toward each other deepening. Noah had worked at headquarters while his arm was healing, while Kit had gone to sea every day aboard the *Osprey*. And every night Noah was there, waiting on the dock for her to disembark. Their weekends were special, spent in the quiet of their home or out at the cove. Their home... Kit smiled to herself. Funny how she thought of everything in the plural now. Their home, their cats and dog.

Her stomach began to roll in warning. Kit put the coffee down and stood. "Excuse me, I'm going down to the cabin."

Noah glanced worriedly over at her. Kit's face had grown pale. "Seasickness?"

"Yes. And right on time. I'll be better around noon, Noah." She smiled lamely into his concerned green eyes. "Don't worry."

An hour later, Noah made his way from the bridge down to his cabin. He knocked once on the bulkhead door and entered. Kit had just emerged from the bathroom, looking waxen.

Grimly he gripped her arm, leading her over to the bunk. "You look like hell," he muttered, going and getting a warm washcloth.

Gratefully Kit took the cloth, wiping her face. "I hate throwing up."

He gave her a fierce look. "Look, something needs to be done about this, Kit. It can't continue. It's bad for your health."

The amount of care in his expression sent her heart soaring with joy. Kit placed her fingers on his arm. "Okay, I'll go to the base dispensary."

"It's about time. Stay home tomorrow and go to a doctor." He tunneled his fingers through her black hair, which now hung shoulder length. He saw Kit's eyes go soft with longing. The need to take her into his arms and make love with her was excruciating. Stilling his desire for her, Noah tucked away those clamoring feelings. When Operation Storm was over, he was going to admit his love for her.

"Okay, okay. I'll take the day off and get to a doctor. But really, Noah, I don't think he'll be able to do much."

He caressed her cheek. "Maybe you're anemic. You never have any color in your face anymore," he muttered.

It was rare that Kit would allow herself the gift of putting her arms around Noah's shoulders and hugging him, but she did now. Closing her eyes, she felt his arms slide around her, and she moaned softly. Their careful avoidance of each other had been torturous. "I'll be okay," she whispered, leaning tiredly against him.

"You'd better be, lady," he growled, pressing a chaste kiss to her hair.

Kit walked into the Coast Guard dispensary at nine the following morning. Feeling wretched with the usual nausea, she carefully made her way between a number of waiting patients. Most of them were pregnant women or worried young mothers coping with their sick charges. Kit found a seat next to a red-haired girl who was obviously pregnant.

The girl, probably no more than nineteen, was dressed in a pink cotton maternity dress and smiled encouragingly over at Kit. "How far along are you?"

"Along?"

The girl ran her fingers across her swollen belly in a loving gesture. "How many months before you have your baby?"

Kit gave her a startled look. "I'm not pregnant. I'm here to see if something can't be done about my seasickness."

The girl gave her a shy smile. "Funny, I thought you were pregnant. You have that look."

"What look?"

"You know what they say about a woman who's with child—her skin becomes real glowing."

Kit smiled gently, taken by the girl's interest in her. "I'm sure it's a case of seasickness."

"You're nauseated now?"

Pressing her hand to her stomach, Kit nodded. "Terribly."

"And you're not on a boat. How could that be seasickness?" she pointed out, still smiling.

Closing her eyes tightly, Kit felt a sinking sensation in the pit of her stomach. My God, she couldn't be pregnant! Not now! Oh, God, not now! Dante still had that contract out on her. She was living on borrowed time until Garcia was captured. But Noah had made beautiful, wonderful love to her a little more than three months ago. And her menstrual cycle was erratic at best because of the stress of her job.

Slowly opening her eyes, Kit stared blankly ahead, her mind whirling with the possible options she'd face if she was pregnant. Hard, terrible choices would have to be made to help her and Noah's child survive the coming confrontation.

Kit heard her name called. Rising, she took a deep breath and grimly threaded her way through the groups of children and their mothers.

"Congratulations, Kit," Dr. Ann Whitten said, coming back into the small room.

"I'm pregnant?"

"Indeed you are," the gray-haired woman said, smiling.

Kit's fingers trembled as she buttoned up her blouse. "How far along am I?" she asked hollowly.

"I'd say three and a half to four months. Further, you're anemic. I'm writing you a prescription for some iron tablets to get your red blood count back up."

Letting out a shaky breath, Kit rubbed her brow. "I can't believe it."

"You need rest, Kit," Dr. Whitten said, coming up and standing in front to her. "You're working too hard."

Kit avoided the doctor's probing gaze. "What happens if I keep working, Doctor?"

"Your uterus is slightly tipped, Kit. If you want to keep that baby, you're going to have to rest. Some women can push hard for nine months and deliver a strapping young tyke, but you can't. With your underweight condition, anemia and a body that isn't fully cooperating in carrying this child, you need rest. And plenty of it.''

Kit drew in a painful breath. She wanted this baby more than life itself. Her gray eyes mirrored the turmoil she was experiencing. ''But if I had to work, Doctor, wouldn't it be better *now* rather than later? I mean, wouldn't my chances of a miscarriage rise if I were farther along in my pregnancy?''

Ann Whitten nodded, placing the clipboard on her desk. ''The farther along you are, Kit, the greater the chance that you may have to opt for total bed rest until your baby's born.''

Silence engulfed them while Kit mulled over her limited options. ''Doctor, there are certain things I have to do in the next couple of months. I don't have a choice.''

Dr. Whitten handed her the prescription. ''There are always choices, Kit. If you want to carry your baby to full term, you'll have to do something to alter the work you feel has to be done.''

Kit touched her brow, anguish filling her heart. If they didn't capture Garcia and Dante, her life would be worthless. Dante had fled the U.S., jumping bail and escaping to Colombia but leaving a contract out on Kit, according to the undercover agent trailing him. She stole a look over at the kind doctor's face. ''You're right,'' she whispered. ''I'll do the best I can.'' Kit slid off the table and stood. Picking up her purse, she decided to visit Chuck Cordeman. Only he could help her now.

* * *

"What the hell are you doing here?" Cordeman demanded as Kit walked into his office.

"We have to talk, Chuck," she announced without preamble. "Let's go into one of the interrogation rooms."

Cordeman reluctantly pushed his football-shaped body out of the dilapidated chair. "You look like hell," he observed.

Kit gave him a bitter smile. "Thanks for the compliment."

Cordeman walked like no one else Kit had ever seen. He seemed to list from side to side. As they moved down a long, poorly lit hallway, she wondered if he would ever get seasick. Probably not, because of the way he mimicked a ship bobbing on the ocean. Chuck was used to that kind of motion.

"Okay, what's so important that you've broken your cover by coming here?" Chuck demanded, pointing to one of two chairs in the small, barren room as he shut the door.

Kit sat down, facing her old boss. "I need some information, Chuck."

"About what?"

"When is Garcia going to move his mother ship?"

He shrugged. "We've got an undercover agent in place and we're hoping to find out soon."

Her heart pounded heavily in her breast. "I've got to know."

Cordeman regarded her darkly. "What's going down, Kit? You look like death warmed over. In fact, you look worse than when you left us. What's Trayhern doing? Working you too hard?''

She bit her lower lip. "No, Chuck. It isn't Noah. I—'' She swallowed hard. "Make me a promise?"

His face softened slightly. "What's wrong, Kit? You're shaking.''

"I need a promise from you first, Chuck," she said, desperation in her voice.

"Okay, okay, I promise. What is it?"

Kit fought back her tears. "Chuck, I'm four months pregnant with Noah's child, and there's a contract out on my head. I know the odds are in Dante's favor of finding me sooner rather than later.'' She reached out, gripping his meaty hand. "Promise me you'll tell no one about my condition,'' she rushed on. "I've got to help find Dante and Garcia before they get to me first.''

Chuck's face betrayed his emotion. His eyes grew round and he stared at her in disbelief. "Oh, God," he muttered. And then he got heavily to his feet, giving her a sorrowful look. "Ah, Kit, why now? Pregnant? Of all the bad timing—''

She blinked back the tears. "Okay, so it was lousy timing, dammit! I didn't plan this, Chuck. It was an accident. But I can't help that now.''

His eyes grew squinty. "Does Trayhern know?"

"No, and he's not going to find out, either. If he knew, he'd never let me continue to participate in Operation Storm.''

Cordeman snorted vehemently. "He'd pack your rear out of Dade County so fast it'd make your head spin. He's protective as hell."

"And getting me out of Dade isn't going to improve my chances of surviving, Chuck. You and I both know that. And you need me to identify Garcia." Kit rubbed her face tiredly. "That's why I ask you, when is Garcia going to make his move? The sooner the better."

"Yeah, no kidding. Damn, Kit, this is bad."

"No one's more aware of that than I am."

"You're not the narc detective I used to know," he muttered, shaking his head sadly. "You're not the tough broad who could be counted on to carry anything through with success. Kit, you've changed." And then he added, "For the better. You're more feminine. More—" Words failed him, and he shifted to his official tone. "Okay," he muttered gruffly, "what do you want me to do? Where are we going with all these confessions?"

Kit gave him a wobbly smile. "The original plan was for me to board the mother ship in search of Garcia and Dante."

"After the scum has been rounded up," he put in.

"But there could be firefights on the mother ship, Chuck. I don't want my baby exposed to gunfire."

"We're bringing several decoy craft piloted by DEA agents into the bay during the trading. They'll be taking the names and registry of drug-buying ships so we can hunt them down later. Knowing Garcia the way I do, I'm betting he won't be on board the *Marie-Elise* during the buying. He'll play it smart and be on a smaller boat hanging somewhere around the bay. How about if you stay on one of our DEA decoys? I'll be boarding the *Marie-Elise* as soon as the bust goes down. I can get in touch with you by radio once we've got everything secured and then you can come on board.''

"That sounds better," Kit answered, relief in her voice. Then she frowned and rubbed her temples, hating herself momentarily. "The last thing I want to do is hold off telling Noah about the baby—" she glanced over at Chuck "—but until Dante and Garcia are identified and behind bars, I'm still on their hit list."

"I understand. You been to a doctor yet?"

She got up, pushing her fingers through her hair in an aggravated motion. "Yes. She said something about me having a tipped uterus and that I stand a good chance of losing my baby if I don't get off my feet soon."

Cordeman grimaced. "Damn, Kit—"

Her eyes were dazed with fatigue. "I don't have a choice, Chuck. I just hope Garcia makes his move soon."

He grunted, getting to his feet. "Makes two of us. Well, come on, let's get you home. You really look wiped out."

Kit walked over and put her arm around Chuck's sloped shoulders. "Thanks," she whispered, meaning it.

He gave her a thin smile. "For what? If Trayhern finds out I knew you were pregnant and didn't pull you out of this operation, *he'll* put a contract out on *me*."

Kit's heart wrenched at the sound of Tripoli's joyous bark. Noah was home. She glanced at the wall clock: 9:00 p.m. Scrubbing the potato with renewed nervous energy, she thought, *God, give me the strength to lie to him. Please, please don't let him see I'm not telling him the whole truth. I have to carry this off! For all of us....*

Noah ambled into the kitchen, a smile on his handsome face. "Are you feeling better?" he asked, coming over to the sink and placing his arms around her.

Kit trembled, shutting her eyes, biting back the words that wanted to flow from her heart. "Better," she said in a strained voice. It was unlike Noah to embrace her like this, but she understood, needing his strength right now.

"Mmm, you smell like jasmine," Noah whispered seductively rocking her gently in his arms. "And you look a hundred percent improved from this morning."

"I just took a bath." That wasn't a lie. She raised her head. Was any man as strong or compassionate as Noah? Her lips parted in unspoken joy as she saw the corners of his mobile, sensual mouth turn up as he gazed down at her. And his eyes...oh, God, she could be forever lost in their changing sea color. Kit saw tenderness in the golden flecks mingled with the green and felt her heart melting with unparalleled joy. The words *I love you* wanted to tear from her. Kit closed her eyes, fighting them back, fighting everything back.

"What did the doctor say?" he asked, splaying his long fingers down her back, gently following the curve of her spine.

Kit took a deep, ragged breath, feeling her heart rip in two, screaming to be released from the bondage of a secret that must be kept buried deeply within her. "She said I was anemic."

Noah eased his embrace, studying her. "How anemic?"

She shrugged, making light of it. "Enough to put me on some iron pills for a while."

"What about the nausea? Anemia doesn't cause that, does it?"

Kit's heart pounded violently to underscore her loathing to betray Noah. "No," she murmured, closing her eyes so that he couldn't see the lie. "She said it was an inner ear imbalance and that nothing could be done about it."

Noah stroked her silky hair, disgruntled. He studied her troubled features. "Could you use some good news then?"

Hurting inwardly at deceiving him, Kit whispered, "Something...anything..."

Noah traced the clean line of her jaw. It was so easy to become lost within the facets of Kit's face. She had a wonderful bone structure, wide-set eyes that were now shadowed with pain and seriousness. Her mouth was one of her most beautiful features, Noah thought.

And he hungered to kiss her. He roused himself from his torrid reverie and realized that Kit was waiting for him to answer her.

"We had just pulled into the dock when we got word from the undercover agent in Colombia that the *Marie-Elise* had heaved anchor. She's in the Gulf of Darien. From the looks of it, she's heading in the direction of the Windward Passage choke point. It's a little early to confirm that yet, but right now it appears to be her bearing."

Kit's knees jellied. "The *Marie-Elise* is—"

Noah watched her cheeks stain with color. "Yeah, Operation Storm is in full gear."

Her prayer had been answered! Kit gasped. "When do we go to the *Osprey*?"

"I've got my crew outfitting her right now. It means a number of days at sea." Noah's features grew worried. "Are you sure you'll be able to take this? It's going to be rough."

Sinking against him, Kit buried her face in his chest. "I'll do whatever it takes, Noah," she whispered. "I just want this part of my life wrapped up."

Noah felt the urgency in her voice, understanding. "I know," he soothed. Holding her away from him, his voice grew husky. "And just as soon as this damned operation is ended, Kit, you and I have some serious talking to do."

She drowned in the darkness of his eyes. There was unspoken warmth in them. "Yes," she said faintly, "we're going to have a long talk...." Now, if only Noah would agree to go along with Chuck's change in plans, she and her baby would be safe. Safe for a future she would die to protect.

"There's been a change in plans, Lieutenant." Cordeman's face was shadowed as he stood at dockside, close to the *Osprey*.

Kit stole a glance at Noah's scowling features. The lighting carved his face into harsh planes.

"What change, Cordeman?" he growled, standing close to Kit.

For a second Cordeman's gaze locked with Kit's. There was a silent exchange and then he broke contact, directing his attention to the officer. "I want Kit safe on the *Guayama*. It's one of our DEA decoy boats that will be tooling around in the bay, getting names and the registry of the dealer doing business. You'll transfer Kit over before pulling into Cap Haitien, which is where Garcia is headed. I'm sending Barnes, one of our narc agents, with her. There's no way in hell I want her life jeopardized on this mission."

Noah's mouth relaxed slightly. "For once we agree on something, Cordeman. You feel Garcia's going to be in a boat hovering near the *Marie-Elise*?"

"That's right. So Kit can use the binoculars to check out the smaller craft, and stay safe."

Nodding, Noah looked toward the *Osprey*. It was nearly one in the morning and time to go. "I like the idea."

Kit started to sway, but caught herself. Relief surged through her as the three of them walked toward the ship. Dawn would bring the confrontation with Garcia. Soon the showdown would come. Shoring up her broken emotions, Kit walked up the plank and stepped onto the *Osprey*. *Hurry,* she prayed. *Hurry and get this over with....*

A bloodred dawn greeted Kit's eyes as she moved up the steel steps toward the bridge of the *Osprey*. Kit found Noah, Cordeman, Edwards and Barnes hunkered over a map spread across the console.

Noah glanced up, his heart wrenching with anxiety. Kit looked ethereal in the dawn's light. "Things are firmed up," he told her. "Come and join us."

Chuck nodded in her direction, a question in his eyes. Kit forced a slight smile for his benefit, wedging herself between Noah and him.

"What's going on?" she asked, her voice still husky with sleep.

Noah pointed to the map, circling the area. "The *Marie-Elise* has dropped anchor in a cove near Cap Haitien." His voice betrayed his aggravation. "Garcia wasn't stupid. The bay is shallow, with little room to maneuver a larger ship. It means that the *Sea Eagle* and the *Osprey* are going to have to choke off the only escape route in or out of the bay. They'll barricade the entrance by positioning the cutters horizontally across it. We aren't going to be able to sail into the bay at all."

A sheen of perspiration showed on Noah's hardened features as he studied the map with fierce intensity. Kit realized timing was critical to capturing the

Marie-Elise and the drug dealers like fish in a net. A shiver shot down her spine and she tried to throw off the cape of dread that settled around her drawn shoulders.

"It's going to be vital that Kit be able to find Garcia," Cordeman said. "With the shallow waters, I'm positive that the bastard will be aboard a smaller boat."

Straightening, Noah studied Kit. "The *Guayama* is already alongside. We'll transfer you and Barnes now, and then Henri Galera, the DEA agent, will take you into the bay. After you're in there, we'll wait until he calls us to take our position to trap all of them."

"Fine," Kit said. She told the crew on the bridge goodbye, and then Noah took her arm, leading her to the lower deck.

Like everyone else, Kit wore a flak jacket and a shoulder holster. The sun had just peeked over the horizon, sending shafts of glaring light across the choppy waters. The tension she felt in Noah put her on edge.

"It will be over soon," she told him.

"No one's happier about it than me," he confided. Stopping at the ladder, he pointed toward a small tug that bobbed beside them. "The *Guayama.*"

The small boat was nothing more than a rusty scow sitting high in the water. Kit saw a black man at the wheel, who waved up at them. "Not much to it, is there?"

"No." Noah turned Kit around, his hands on her shoulders. He didn't give a damn who saw them at that instant. Fear hovered around him, and he couldn't shake the feeling. He wasn't sure if it was for him or Kit. "Listen, you be damn careful, Kitten," he rasped, holding her gaze.

"I'll be very careful, darling."

His face relaxed slightly. He couldn't kiss her. He couldn't tell her he loved her—yet. There was a slight tremble to his voice. "Stay safe. We've got everything to live for."

Barnes came walking up. Kit couldn't hide her disappointment. She had wanted to kiss Noah one last time. But that was impossible now. "I'll see you when this is all over, Noah. Please, *you* be careful."

Releasing her arms, Noah stepped back. He gave her a warm smile meant only for her. "Very careful, Kitten."

Turning away, Kit stepped distractedly down the steel ladder and took Galera's waiting hand.

"Welcome aboard, Detective Anderson."

Kit stepped aside, allowing Barnes to board. "Thank you, Henri." Her eyes lifted upward, and she saw Noah standing far above them, silhouetted by the growing light, his face grim. Anguish overwhelmed Kit. Out of habit, she touched her stomach. Was it because she was pregnant that she was more fearful than usual? Dread stalked her. Every time she felt that ugly sensation crawling through her, it meant danger.

"Cast off!" Galera ordered Barnes, who released the lines to the *Osprey*.

A lump formed in Kit's throat. She raised her hand. Noah raised his in return. Tears blurred his stalwart figure and Kit turned away, no longer able to stand the pain of their separation. Heading to the bridge, where Galera was, Kit wanted to focus all her attention on the forthcoming bust. Her life, the life of her baby and Noah's, depended on it.

"There they are," Henri said grimly as they moved into the shallow cove.

The *Marie-Elise* was anchored as close to the shoreline as possible, lying heavy in the water. Clusters of boats bobbed next to one another at the ship's starboard side as huge bales of marijuana were crane-hoisted onto the smaller ones.

Kit counted at least fifty smaller boats in the cove. Taking the binoculars, she began to scan the *Marie-Elise*. She heard Henri make a call to alert both Coast Guard cutters to come in and close off escape from the bay. In half an hour they would arrive on station, and then all hell would break loose.

"Man, they're doing a booming business," Henri said with a chuckle. His skin glistened with perspiration.

People in ragtag outfits of gaily colored shirts and jeans were running up and down metal stairs at the bottom of the loading platform of the *Marie-Elise*. "I don't see Garcia or Dante," Kit muttered. As soon as one boat was loaded, another zipped up to take its place. Her heart pounded with anxiety as she continued to make a slow, thorough appraisal of each boat near the mother ship. Where were they? She saw flags of all nationalities being flown.

Henri glanced at his watch. "In ten minutes the Coast Guard will be on station," he warned, maneuvering the chugging tug toward the beach to get a closer look at another group of boats anchored there. "Take a look at this next bunch, Kit."

She swung her binoculars toward the shore. There were more than thirty sleek inboard cruisers, beat-up rusty tubs and yachts huddled together, all waiting their turn to get the bales. Could she spot Garcia and Dante before the Coast Guard closed off the cove? Tension thrummed through her as she frantically searched each boat in turn.

"Five more minutes," Henri warned, "before these boats split like a flock of startled birds. The moment they see the Coast Guard, they're gonna panic." He gave the wooden wheel a hefty turn, urging the *Guayama* around so that the bow was aimed at the mother ship.

Kit glanced up; the shore was no more than fifty feet away from them.

Barnes crowded in on the bridge, unholstering his revolver and releasing the safety. "Man, this is going to be a mess in a few minutes. Where are all these boats going to go when they find out they're all trapped?"

Chortling, Galera asked, "You ever seen druggies walk on water?"

Kit grinned sickly, continuing to rapidly scan the boats. Suddenly her heart thudded. "Oh, my God!" she breathed. "It's them. Garcia! And Dante!"

"Where?" Henri demanded.

"Over there," Kit said, pointing. "That red-and-white charter boat about two hundred yards east of us." Her throat ached with renewed fear as Barnes took the binoculars.

Henri grabbed the microphone, calling the *Osprey* and *Sea Eagle*, giving them a clear description of the boat. Kit listened in stunned silence, watching the boat. Her pulse was strong, her heart beating wildly in her breast.

"They're sitting on two-hundred-fifty horsepower of boat," Barnes growled, lowering the binoculars.

"They ain't gonna go anywhere," Henri said with a booming laugh. He glanced at his watch and then over his shoulder. "They're here."

Kit jerked her attention to the only entrance to the cove. Both the Coast Guard vessels had just hoved into view, stationing themselves like a barrier across it. She turned back to the smugglers. Suddenly, without warning, the entire cove rippled with fear. Kit saw smugglers sprint into action as soon as they saw the *Osprey* and *Sea Eagle*. Shouting and cursing filled the air. It was as if a huge tidal wave had smashed through the cove. Boats fled in all directions.

All her attention was riveted on the red-and-white boat. Suddenly the huge, thunderous engines roared to life, water foaming and swirling madly around the rear of the boat. From the corner of her eye, Kit saw four other DEA boats of varying sizes, shapes and power closing in on Garcia to cut him off and surround him. Henri thrust the two throttles forward, causing the little *Guayama* to leap ahead with surprising adroitness. They were closing the net around Garcia.

Barnes cursed and gripped Kit's shoulder. "Look out!" he screamed. "He's trying to escape!"

Kit's lips parted, a cry lurching from her throat. In the blinding split seconds that followed, the red-and-white monster of a boat careened wildly, its bow pointed directly at the *Guayama*, which blocked its only remaining route of escape.

The snarl of engines and the sudden crunching sound of bows meeting, folding and cracking shattered the air. Kit was thrown heavily against Barnes, who was slammed into the rear bulkhead. The explosion that followed punctured the cove like an artillery barrage.

Kit remembered wave after wave of broiling heat from the explosion, screams, then the smell of diesel fuel in the air. She crawled to her hands and knees, blood dribbling from her nose and mouth. Water rushed into the destroyed bridge of the listing *Guayama*. Blindly she reached out, gripping Barnes's limp arm. She yelled at him, realizing in her dazed condition that he was unconscious.

Staggering to her feet, Kit turned. Nausea overwhelmed her and she jerked her head away, unable to cope with the grisly scene that met her eyes. Henri was dead. But Barnes was still alive. Kit heard gunshots all around them, ignored the angry firing and dragged the agent off the bridge and onto the deck of the sinking *Guayama*.

Barnes revived just in time. Kit stared disbelievingly as diesel fuel and fire raced across the surface around the two wrecked boats. She gasped for breath, realizing that several people were flailing nearby in the water, all of them heading for shore to escape.

"Come on!" she begged Barnes. She jerked his arm, and they both jumped overboard.

The water was surprisingly warm, and Kit coughed wildly, floundering toward shore. The heavy flak jacket weighed her down, and she swallowed water as she struggled to stay afloat. Barnes was having equal trouble. They touched bottom minutes later.

Kit's hair hung limply around her face as she staggered toward the beach, Barnes weaving unsteadily on his feet in front of her.

"Kit!" Barnes screamed in warning.

Automatically Kit flattened, throwing herself into the shallow water as the crack of a gun sounded very close to her. Barnes was thrown backward into the water, a red stain moving across his head. Kit rolled on her side, fumbling to unsnap the revolver that rested beneath her left armpit.

"Hold it!" a voice snarled.

Her hand froze on the gun and Kit looked up. Into the viperous eyes of Emilio Dante.

Chapter Twelve

Cordeman was the first to discover what had occurred. It had been one of the many messages coming across the bridge of the *Osprey*. He had seen the two boats collide close to shore and heard the resulting earsplitting explosion. Moving with unaccustomed quickness, Cordeman got a ride on another DEA decoy boat and made it over to the *Marie-Elise* to locate Noah and his boarding crew.

Cordeman found Trayhern, his face blackened by grime and sweat, down in the hold. He grabbed Noah's arm and jerked him around to get his full attention. The roar of several fire hoses and shouts of the men directing water on the blaze mingled with Cordeman's raised voice.

"Kit's in trouble!"

Noah wiped a trail of sweat from his eyes, blinking once. "What?"

Cordeman's grip tightened. "The boat Kit was on was rammed by Garcia and Dante!"

Noah's mouth opened and closed. He stared disbelievingly at Cordeman. Everything had happened so fast. The boarding party from the *Osprey* had been the first to engage in gunfire, and he had led the initial attack aboard the bristling mother ship. He pointed toward the hold ladder.

"Get topside so I can hear you," Noah ordered. He turned, giving orders to Chief Stanton to continue battling the blaze, then quickly climbed the ladder. He took a deep breath of clean air, and his eyes pinned the narc supervisor.

"What the hell are you talking about, Cordeman?"

"We got a call from the *Guayama* seconds before it was rammed. Kit spotted Garcia and Dante on a red-and-white charter boat near them." He gritted his teeth, watching the officer's face pale beneath the tan. "I don't know if they rammed the *Guayama* on purpose or not. Anyway, an agent on one of the other DEA decoy boats watched the whole thing through binoculars. With Galera's description, he was able to identify Garcia and Dante."

Noah felt his heart tearing apart inside his chest, and he looked toward shore, where two vessels were still mated and burning from their collision. "No—" he croaked. "No!"

"Get hold of yourself, Trayhern! They saw Kit, Barnes and Dante make it to shore. Dante shot Barnes and he took Kit prisoner."

Noah tensed and glared toward the scenic beach lined with palm trees. Beyond the grove of palms, the rocky land rose sharply, dotted with gnarled trees and cactus. He swung around.

"He'll kill her."

"Not yet. She's his ticket to safety until he can get to the other side of the hill above us," Chuck growled. "Come on, let's get a rescue party together. If Dante reaches some means of safety before we can get to him, he will kill Kit."

Grimly Noah tightened his lips to a thin line of pain. "What about Garcia?"

"Dead. We just recovered his and Galera's body from the area of the collision."

Noah uttered an expletive and moved quickly toward the debarkation area. Cordeman reached out, pulling him to a halt. "Look, there's one more thing you gotta know before we try to rescue Kit."

"What?" Noah snarled, tired of Cordeman feeding him bits and pieces of information. All he wanted to do was find Kit. He glared at Cordeman, confused by the look on the man's sweaty face.

"I promised her I wouldn't tell you." He breathed harshly, mopping his brow with his handkerchief.

"But things didn't go right. Trayhern, she's four months pregnant with your baby."

Stunned, Noah froze. *Four months pregnant?* Tears welled in his eyes. "When?"

Cordeman swore. "I don't know what your love life's like! You answer those questions, dammit. She went to the doctor recently and it was confirmed." His voice lost its angry tone as he saw the officer's face turn ashen. "Look," he went on, "the doc told her she'd have a tough time carrying the baby to full term." He mopped his brow nervously. "Dammit, what I'm trying to tell you is that even if we're able to rescue Kit, she still might be in serious danger of a miscarriage!"

Shakily Noah touched his brow, trying to force his crowded, cartwheeling thoughts into some semblance of order. Kit was pregnant with his child! A deluge of joy was shattered by terror for her and the baby's life. He had to think straight! He could not allow his emotions to get the better of him. "Yeah... okay," he muttered, forcing himself to think, not feel. "Come on, we'll get a boarding party together."

Noah's green eyes were dark with despair as he looked around at the group of six volunteers. Each man's face was tense, anticipating. They all knew the score—Dante would use Kit as a shield, kill her at the first opportunity and escape. Further, she was pregnant, and even if they could find Dante, it might be too late. Noah made sure a corpsman came along, just in case, and a helicopter from a hospital in Port-au-Prince was on its way.

Two Haitian drug agents would guide the party ashore and help them track Dante. They knew their island better than anyone and were aware of all the nooks and crannies in the rocky foothills that loomed above the beach. Noah tried to shove aside his personal suffering, but it was impossible. He rubbed his grimy, sweat-streaked face, fighting to keep his escaping emotions under control. Picking up his M-16 and jamming the baseball cap back on his head, he growled, "All right, let's get Dante."

Dante wheezed brokenly, giving Kit a push that sent her sprawling on the hillside. He rested the gun on his knee as he sat for a minute and tried to catch his breath. Glaring at her, he snarled, "Don't move, or I'll blow your damned head off your shoulders."

Kit sobbed for breath and dragged herself into a sitting position. She dared not speak back to Dante, dared not aggravate him into shooting her as he had Barnes. How far had they come in the past half hour? Turning her head, she saw the chaos down below them in the small, cluttered cove. Smoke was still pouring in thick black clouds from the *Marie-Elise*. Fear made Kit tremble as she sought to fight down the panic eating at the edges of her mind. Dante had jerked her up by her hair, forcing her to run out of the water toward the line of palm trees on the beach. Once there, he kept shoving the snub nose of the gun into her back and forcing her to keep running up into the hills. Her hands and knees were bleeding where she had fallen several times, trying to scramble up the steep slopes. And Dante was close to losing what little patience he had.

Kit weakly leaned her head against her drawn-up knees, gasping for breath. Her clothes clung to her sweaty body. She was a hostage, she realized bleakly. *Dante will keep me alive for as long as I'm useful to him.* Tears stung her eyes and she fought against a burgeoning sob caught in her throat. Dante despised weakness in any form.

"Damn!" Dante swore, leaping to his feet. His narrow face hardened, his brown eyes growing black.

Kit jerked her head up, following his gaze. Down below on the beach was a contingent of men armed with rifles. Her heart soared as she recognized Noah among them. Tears drifted down her dirty cheeks as she also saw Chuck Cordeman with the group. They knew! Someone had spotted Dante taking her prisoner! Hope escalated with fear. Wildly Kit glanced over at Dante's ferretlike face. A snarl had lifted his thin lips away from his small, sharply pointed teeth. He looked like a snake ready to strike. He turned slowly, his opaque eyes burning into her.

"Get up," he demanded coldly.

Kit rose, unsure of what he was capable of doing next. Her mind spun with options, choices. How fast could Noah and his squad move? Would it take them the same amount of time to traverse the trail she and

Dante had taken? Kit doubted it. She watched as Dante raised the ugly black barrel of the gun toward her.

"You'd better pray you can run even harder, Anderson, because that's what we're going to do. I ain't lettin' the Coast Guard catch me."

Kit stifled a scream, watching as his finger stroked the trigger. Her throat was parched, dehydration stalking her thirsty body. Her only ounce of satisfaction was that Dante was going to be equally deprived of water. Hopefully this would slow him down enough so that Noah could reach them in time. "I'll do the best I can," she rasped.

Dante cursed, motioning for her to turn around. "Shut up and get moving!" He jabbed the barrel savagely into her neck. "I'm gonna enjoy puttin' you down, Anderson. All I need to do is find a boat on the other side of that cliff, and then you're dead meat."

Noah wasn't aware of anything except catching up with Kit. Those few moments watching her struggle up the hill with Dante on her heels made his stomach turn. Leaping over a series of vines, he pushed his body to its maximum, disregarding the pain in his lungs and the stinging sensation of cacti as it tore at his lower legs. *I love you, Kit! Just keep going, don't try anything with Dante. Just survive! Survive!*

Kit sobbed for breath, feeling the punch of the gun barrel in her bruised back again. Dante cursed her, giving her a shove forward.

"Keep moving!" he panted.

Sweat blinded her, and she stumbled over another vine. The summit to the hill seemed so far away. And the heat . . . she heard Dante gasping behind her. The man must be made out of steel, she thought. He never slowed down. They reached an outcropping of granite eight feet high with gaping fissures, which crowned their escape point in front of them. They would have to either go around it, losing precious time, or try to climb it. Kit turned, eyeing Dante. He cursed, having come to the same conclusion as her.

He glanced over his shoulder. The six men in uniform were climbing steadily toward them. Dante probably had five shots left in his revolver, Kit thought. It wouldn't pay him to fire wildly at this distance. The rescue party would take cover in the rocks, completely safe from his useless attack.

"We're gonna climb this face and save time. If I find a boat down in that harbor once we're on the other side of this hill, I won't need you any longer."

Kit gasped, leaning over and trying to recover her breath.

She raised her chin, a sheen of sweat on her flushed face. A dull ache was beginning in her lower abdomen, sending a thread of fear through her. She placed her hand across her belly, anguish clearly written on her face. *No . . . no,* her heart screamed. She tried to concentrate on Dante and on giving Noah a clear shot at him. If the drug dealer foolishly decided to climb the rock wall, he would become an obvious target for an M-16 rifle. It was a long shot, Kit realized. If her blurred memory served her correctly, even a SWAT team sharpshooter couldn't place a bull's-eye at over six hundred yards. And right now, if she estimated accurately, Noah was at least eight hundred yards behind them. Would he try anyway? It would be her last chance before they started up the cliff that led down to the other cove.

More pain shot raggedly up through the center of her body and Kit doubled over, dropping to her knees. Tears squeezed from beneath her lids as she wrapped her arms around her middle, her head resting against the dirt and stones.

Dante growled. "Get up! Dammit, get up! We're climbing. You first!"

Kit gasped, lifting her head, tears streaking down her cheeks, making silvery paths through the dirt. Dante's eyes were wild as he waved the gun at her head. "I—I can't!"

He gripped her shoulder, his long fingers digging into her flesh. Placing the revolver at her temple, he snarled, "I said, get up."

The pain increased as Kit swayed to her feet. She tottered toward the wall, blindly lifting her foot into the first crevice, finding a handhold above her. Tears blurred her vision as she hoisted herself upward. Her baby—oh, God, her baby...the pain...no, it couldn't happen! *Don't let me lose our baby....*

"Hurry up!" Dante shrilled, climbing right up behind her.

Kit forced herself to take another step and then another up the face of the cliff, sweat rolling down her brow. Her hands were bloodied and scraped as she hunted frantically for another handhold above her. Dante jabbed the revolver repeatedly into her lower back. *Noah!* she screamed in her mind. *Please take a shot at Dante. Hurry! Please, hurry!*

Noah made a slashing motion with his hand, a silent order for his men to halt behind him. He dropped to one knee. He had his target. He saw Dante start to climb the wall. His heart was pounding achingly in his chest as he wrapped the sling of the M-16 around his upper arm, steadying the rifle, willing his body to stop trembling so he could draw a bead. What direction was the wind coming from? And how many knots? He knew from much experience with weapons that wind direction played a key role in the trajectory of a bullet. If he estimated windage incorrectly, the bullet could easily strike Kit, instead. Or, he could miss Dante completely, and he and Kit would be over the wall before he could fire off another careful shot. Sweat stung his eyes. His face hardened, his mouth pursed as he raised the rifle into position. *Stop breathing. Don't move. Kit—Kit, I love you.* His finger squeezed back against the trigger, and he increased the pressure, willing the rifle barrel to remain steady despite the agony tearing through his heart.

* * *

Kit heard Dante swear directly below her. She gripped the granite, hugging the rock surface as pain arched through the core of her body, blanking everything else from her mind. Somewhere in the haze of agony, she heard the crack of a rifle in the humid afternoon air. Dante let out a groan and dropped to the ground.

Gasping with relief, Kit sobbed, unable to hold on any longer, the pain tearing at her, robbing her of all senses. It felt as if she were falling in slow motion, and when she hit the earth below it was like hitting a lumpy mattress. Rolling onto her side, Kit curled into a tight ball, feeling the warmth of blood flowing down her legs. A scream tore from her as she frantically tried to keep the baby whose life hung in precarious balance within her trembling, exhausted body. Blackness engulfed her.

Noah scrambled the last three hundred feet ahead of everyone else, leaping over the unmoving Dante to where Kit lay. When he'd seen her fall, it had torn him apart. They had called immediately for helicopter assistance, and even now, as he knelt at her side, he could hear the whapping rotor blades puncturing the air as the helicopter sped toward them.

Noah's hands trembled as he leaned over, barely touching Kit's shoulder. His eyes blurred with tears as he saw blood staining the legs of her jeans, and knew...knew what was happening. Her face was pale, tense even in unconsciousness, her arms wrapped protectively around her belly.

A sob tore from him as he dropped his rifle and gathered Kit into his arms. More sobs wrenched from deep within him as he held her while the chopper sat down on the small landing area below the cliff. Gently picking her up, Noah carried her to the helicopter and the waiting medics on board. The two men quickly laid her on a gurney. Noah climbed into the helicopter, positioning himself near Kit's head. No one said anything as tears drifted down his face. The engine whined and the helicopter lifted off, heading for Port-au-Prince.

Noah watched in silent horror as the two medics worked in unison. Kit lay unconscious in the severely limited space. The roar of the engine, the heaving, bucking motion of the aircraft in the thermals increased his anxiety as Noah watched them put a blood pressure cuff on her left arm. He placed a hand on Kit's head.

"Not good!" the first medic shouted to the second. "Seventy over fifty."

"Dammit!" the second medic yelled, ripping open a pouch containing an IV.

No, Noah thought. *Don't die on me, Kit. Don't.* His hand tightened against her shoulder as he stared down at her colorless features. Tears coursed down his face and he sobbed at his helplessness as she lay bleeding. His own brush with death rushed back to him. He remembered lying on that dark deck, the life draining out of him. Noah jerked his chin up, glaring at the medics, who labored to stabilize her condition.

"She's pregnant," Noah shouted over the din of the closest medic. "Can you save the baby?"

Sweat beaded the medic's forehead as he shot a glance up at the officer. "Don't ask for miracles. I'll be lucky to save her!"

"No!"

"We're doing all we can!"

Noah swallowed back a cry of sheer terror. "Then do more!" he screamed above the earsplitting sounds of the helicopter.

The medic shoved a second IV into Kit's other arm and took another blood pressure reading. Noah watched as the chief medic twisted around to the pilots.

"Blood!" he yelled at them. "Tell the hospital to stand by with whole blood! We can't stabilize her!"

Noah groaned and leaned over, resting his sweaty brow against Kit's limp hair. "No," he begged hoarsely. "Don't leave me, Kit. I love you! Fight back, dammit! You hear me? Fight back!" His hands dug into her shoulders as he willed his own vital force to flow into her limp body.

Wave after wave of agony flowed through Kit, from the bottom of her feet up to her head. It felt like one engulfing, hot, searing pain after another. The pain centered in her lower abdomen, and in that hazy in-between state that straddles consciousness, a moan slipped from her throat. Weakly she tried to raise her hand to place it against her body. Strong, cool fingers caught her hand in midair, captured it and gently brought it back down to her side. Strength. The word, the sensation, imprinted itself on her confused state as she fought to surface, to regain consciousness. The pain reminded her of her baby. A baby who had been created out of love. A frown formed on her brow and she moved her head slowly from side to side as if to deny what her aching body was telling her.

"No," Kit mewed weakly, "no . . ."

A cool hand touched her brow and she felt some semblance of steadiness. Kit stopped mumbling and concentrated on that hand that stroked her hair, bringing a balm to her tortured state. "My baby . . . my baby."

As he leaned closer, Noah's features reflected the anguish he heard in Kit's voice. He glanced up at the doctor standing on the other side of her bed.

The physician gave a brief nod. "Just stay with her, Lieutenant Trayhern. She's regaining consciousness. I'll send a nurse to check on her in half an hour. If you need anything, just press that buzzer."

Tiredly Noah sank into a chair next to Kit's bed. "She'll be okay now?" he asked. His voice was a monotone; it sounded as if it belonged to someone else.

"She lost over two pints of blood, Lieutenant. For someone in her condition, that's plenty. We've replaced the blood. The rest is up to her body. She'll be coming around shortly. Just stay with her."

Noah anxiously searched Kit's pale features. Had it been only two hours ago that he had held her on that rocky outcrop far above the ocean? He wiped his watering, bloodshot eyes and searched her taut face. *Kitten, sweet, harmless kitten. I love you. No matter what happens now, just know I love you.* His long fingers trembled as he stroked her cheek in a caressing gesture meant to give comfort. Kit had almost died.

He shut his eyes tightly, more tears squeezing from beneath his dark lashes. She could have been cold-bloodedly murdered by Dante, who was now dead. Or if he'd missed the long-range shot, Kit could easily have been killed by Noah himself.

A ragged sigh tore from Noah as he raised his head and studied her in the dim light. He cupped her cheek and leaned over, placing a small, tremulous kiss on her cool, unmoving lips. So much else could have happened. But she was alive, and he was alive, and the threat of Garcia and Dante had finally been removed.

"Come back," he called softly, "Kit, come back. Come on, be here with me. It's all right, honey. I love you."

Noah's voice penetrated the fog that enveloped Kit. She opened and then closed her mouth. The name Noah formed on her lips. Her eyelids were simply too heavy to raise, but she felt his mouth upon hers: warmth against cold, life against death, love against loneliness. Another tidal wave of pain forced her into a greater state of wakefulness. A moan came from deep within her throat.

"Noah?"

"Right here, Kit."

His voice was unsteady and thick with tears. Her own tears slid down the sides of her face and soaked into the black hair at her temples. Slowly Kit opened her left hand, clasping Noah's strong, warm one. She forced her eyes open, and saw that Noah's skin was tautly drawn over his cheekbones, the corners of his mouth tucked in with pain, and his eyes...oh, God, his eyes mirrored anguish.

More tears slid down her cheeks and Noah made an effort to dry them with his fingers. Kit forced herself to turn her head. The pain was so great that it hurt to move.

"The pain's worse?" he asked in a hushed voice.

Kit bit down on her lip, barely managing a nod. "Noah—our baby..." she cried softly, gripping his hands. "Our baby...did I lose her?"

Noah leaned close, kissing her tear-soaked lashes, his breath moist against her face. "You're still carrying our baby, honey. It was close. The doctors say you have to be very still and rest." He carefully gathered her limp form into his arms, holding her gently. "I love you so much, Kit," he rasped. "I have for the longest time, but I couldn't say anything." He kissed her damp temple. "Neither of us could admit it."

Relief jagged through Kit. Their baby was safe! She was too weak to lift her arms to put them around Noah's shoulders, but she rested her hands against his arms. "I love you," she whispered.

As carefully as he could, Noah laid Kit back down. He rested one arm near her shoulder, his other hand stroking her hair. Her eyes were like soft gray diamonds. "You're going to be the mother of our child, Kitten." His voice caught. "There's nothing else I want in this world but the two of you. Understand?"

Kit closed her eyes. "I—I lied to you, Noah—"

"I know why you lied, honey. And I understand."

Her eyes widened as his hushed words were soaked up into her heart. He was telling her the truth. Kit could see hope flickering in the depths of his green gaze. Her heart contracted with relief, with love for his understanding. "I had to make sure Garcia and Dante were apprehended, or we'd never have a life of our own. I—I thought I was going to die out on that cliff, Noah. How did you know what happened in the cove?"

He took a deep, unsteady breath. "Chuck told me everything. Including the fact that you were pregnant. I know you tried to do the best you could under the circumstances." Admiration shone in his eyes. "You possess a kind of courage I've rarely seen, Kit."

She closed her eyes, moving her hand across her belly. "Not courage," she said softly, slurring the words. "I fell in love with you, Noah, and I wanted a decent life for us. My courage was nothing more than surviving to make that dream come true.''

Noah stood there, watching her fall into a deep, uninterrupted sleep. Gently he placed his larger hand over her smaller one covering her abdomen. ''Always dream for us,'' he told her softly.

Epilogue

A mournful meow split the quiet of the house. Kit gasped, rushing from the kitchen and hurrying into the living room, wiping her damp hands on her apron.

"Melody Sue Trayhern!" she scolded softly. Stifling a laugh, Kit lifted her fifteen-month-old daughter into her arms, rescuing Tuna Boat from further attack.

Tuna lifted her head, offering Kit a pitiful look that asked, *Why won't she leave me alone?* Kit returned her attention to her dark-haired daughter, ready to deliver a gentle reprimand. But one look into those wide, heart-stealing green eyes and Kit relented as usual. Nuzzling Melody, she gave her a kiss on the cheek and held her tightly to her chest.

"What am I going to do with you, squirt?" she whispered, smiling down at her. Kit was forever stunned by how much Melody resembled Noah. It was true that Melody had Kit's black hair, but those wide, guileless green eyes and her laughter-filled smile were Noah's. Kit scowled, trying to make her daughter realize that she couldn't keep stalking Tuna Boat.

"Now listen, young lady, you're not supposed to pick on poor blind cats. Do you hear me?"

"Kitty?"

Kit suppressed a smile that was begging to be released. "Yes, kitty. You pet her, Melody. Tuna Boat isn't one of your stuffed animals, honey. She's alive and sometimes she doesn't want to be held, even if you want to hold her."

Melody's attention zeroed in on the front door as it opened. Kit rolled her eyes. Everything she had just said to Melody had gone in one ear and out the other! But her smile broadened as she saw Noah step into the foyer. Her heart somersaulted, as it always did, when he greeted her with that devastating smile of welcome.

Kit rocked Melody in her arms, watching as Noah eased through the tangle of welcoming animals. He dropped his hat on the desk and made his way down the hall, careful where he placed his feet. She marveled at how much more handsome he had become with each day, each month of their marriage.

"What's this, a conspiracy in the living room?" he teased, leaning over and placing a kiss on Kit's lips. He lingered a moment longer. "Mmm, you taste good, Mrs. Trayhern. You been nibbling on an apple, maybe?" His green eyes glimmered with a tender smile.

"It's about all I can keep down."

Noah placed his arm around Kit, leaning over her shoulder and ruffling his daughter's curly hair. "What have you been up to, Melody?" he asked, lifting one tiny hand. "Gray cat fur?" And then he raised an eyebrow, giving a very unhappy Tuna Boat an understanding look.

"She was after Tunie—again," Kit muttered, handing Noah his daughter. "Here, you talk to her while I finish getting our supper ready."

Noah hugged Melody with a fierce growl. His daughter squealed with delight, stretching her arms upward. Noah held Melody at arm's length as he followed Kit into the kitchen.

"Tuna is not a stuffed toy," he told her, planting a kiss on her brow.

Melody giggled, happy to be nestled against her father's broad shoulder, her small, pudgy arm encircling his neck. Noah gave his daughter a good-natured smile. He slipped his free arm around Kit's waist as she stood at the drain board, making his nightly salad to accompany his meal.

"How are you feeling?" he asked, some of the teasing leaving his voice.

Kit felt her heart contract with love as he pulled her against his strong, steady body. Closing her eyes, she allowed him to take her full weight for a moment.

"Exhausted," she admitted, and then lifted her chin, meeting his worried gaze. "But deliriously happy."

A smile edged his sensual mouth. "It's getting close to the fourth month. That nausea ought to be stopping soon. You can't keep eating apples and crackers forever."

She grinned. "Have I turned into one yet?"

Leaning down, Noah placed a kiss on her parting lips. "Never," he whispered against her. "But you do taste sweet." He inhaled her feminine fragrance and sighed deeply. "God, how I love you," he told her thickly.

Melody squirmed, giggling in Noah's arm and forcing him to give her all his attention. Noah spotted Tuna Boat at the kitchen entrance and a gleam came to his eye. Putting Melody down, he pointed toward Tuna.

"Go pet kitty for a moment, squirt," he urged, winking up at Kit, who was standing there shaking her head.

"Kitty?"

"That's right, honey. Go pet Tunie. She'll love it."

Happily Melody toddled through the kitchen calling, "Kitty, kitty, kitty...."

With an unhappy yowl, Tuna Boat promptly did an about-face and left for parts unknown.

Kit dried her hands on the apron and then threw her arms around Noah's shoulders. "You're terrible! Using poor Tunie like that." She laughed, pressing her body against his hard length.

Noah grinned, leaning down, claiming her lips in a hot, provocative kiss that made her entire body yearn with desire for him. He drew away, laughter lurking in the depths of his sea-green eyes. "I guess I should feel guilty."

"But you don't."

Grinning, he said, "No, I don't."

Kit gave him a warning look. "That smart little daughter of ours is going to catch on to your trickery, Noah Trayhern."

Noah produced an innocent expression. "All I'm doing is practicing military tactics—a diversionary measure for a moment so I can take my beautiful, pregnant wife into my arms for a well-deserved welcome home kiss."

She laughed with him as he rocked her gently in his arms. "One of these days your deceit is going to be rewarded," she threatened softly, nuzzling his ear.

A low growl vibrated from within him as he ran his splayed fingers down across her swelling belly. His mouth caressed her awaiting lips, tasting deeply of her. Finally he drew away, his green eyes stormy with desire. "We're going to be rewarded again for the love we hold for each other, Kitten," he said huskily.

Her black lashes fell against her flushed cheeks and a sigh of happiness escaped her wet, throbbing lips.

One month after nearly losing her life and Melody, they had been married. And four months after that, their daughter had been born. Kit sighed in memory of those beautiful months waiting for her child. Noah had been with her in the delivery room, and the tears they'd shed together had been ones of pure happiness. Noah was life. He gave life. He shared it with her, Melody and now another baby, who rested within her body. When Kit reopened her eyes, they shimmered with unshed tears and met his deep, loving gaze. "Living with you is all the reward I'll ever need, darling," she told him in a trembling voice filled with love.

Noah's embrace tightened, and he held her, never wanting to let her go. "Never stop dreaming for us, Kitten," he said, kissing her gently.

* * * * *

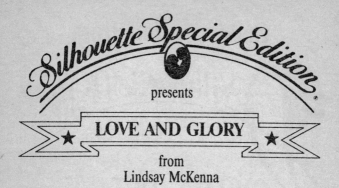

Silhouette Special Edition

presents

★ LOVE AND GLORY ★

from
Lindsay McKenna

Introducing a gripping new series celebrating our men—and women—in uniform. Meet the Trayherns, a military family as proud and colorful as the American flag, a family fighting the shadow of dishonor, a family determined to triumph—with **LOVE AND GLORY!**

June: **A QUESTION OF HONOR** (SE #529) leads the fast-paced excitement. When Coast Guard officer Noah Trayhern offers Kit Anderson a safe house, he unwittingly endangers his own guarded emotions.

July: **NO SURRENDER** (SE #535) Navy pilot Alyssa Trayhern's assignment with arrogant jet jockey Clay Cantrell threatens her career—and her heart—with a crash landing!

August: **RETURN OF A HERO** (SE #541) Strike up the band to welcome home a man whose top-secret reappearance will make headline news . . . with a delicate, daring woman by his side.

Coming in July from

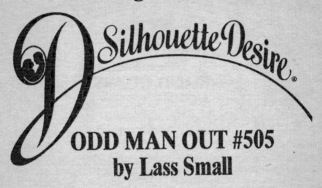

Silhouette Desire

ODD MAN OUT #505
by Lass Small

*Roberta Lambert is too busy with her job to notice that her
new apartment-mate is a strong, desirable man. But Graham
Rawlins has ways of getting her undivided attention....*

Roberta is one of five fascinating Lambert sisters. She is as
enticing as each one of her three sisters, whose stories you have
already enjoyed or will want to read:

- Hillary in GOLDILOCKS AND THE BEHR (Desire #437)

- Tate in HIDE AND SEEK (Desire #453)

- Georgina in RED ROVER (Desire #491)

Watch for Book IV of Lass Small's terrific miniseries and read
Fredricka's story in TAGGED (Desire #528) coming in
October.

1989
IS THE YEAR
OF THE MAN!

What makes a romance? A special man, of course, and Silhouette Desire celebrates that fact with *twelve* of them! From Mr. January to Mr. December, every month has a tribute to the Silhouette Desire hero—our **MAN OF THE MONTH!**

Sexy, macho, charming, irritating . . . irresistible! Nothing can stop these men from sweeping you away. Created by some of your favorite authors, each man is custom-made for pleasure—*reading* pleasure—so don't miss a single one.

Mr. July is Graham Rawlins in ODD MAN OUT by Lass Small
Mr. August is Jeremy Kincaid in MOUNTAIN MAN by Joyce Thies
Mr. September is Clement Cornelius Barto in BEGINNER'S LUCK by Dixie Browning
Mr. October is James Branigan in BRANIGAN'S TOUCH by Leslie Davis Guccione
Mr. November is Shiloh Butler in SHILOH'S PROMISE by BJ James
Mr. December is Tad Jackson in WILDERNESS CHILD by Ann Major

So get out there and find your man!

Silhouette Desire's

MAN OF THE MONTH . . .

MOM-1R

"GIVE YOUR HEART TO SILHOUETTE" SWEEPSTAKES
OFFICIAL RULES

NO PURCHASE NECESSARY TO ENTER OR RECEIVE A PRIZE

1. To enter and join the Silhouette Reader Service, rub off the concealment device on all game tickets. This will reveal the potential value for each Sweepstakes entry number and the number of free books(s) you will receive. Accepting the free book(s) will automatically entitle you to also receive a free bonus gift. If you do not wish to take advantage of our introduction to the Silhouette Reader Service but wish to enter the Sweepstakes only, rub off the concealment device on tickets #1-3 only. To enter, return your entire sheet of tickets. Incomplete and/or inaccurate entries are not eligible for that section or section (s) of prizes. Not responsible for mutilated or unreadable entries or inadvertent printing errors. Mechanically reproduced entries are null and void.

2. Either way, your Sweepstakes numbers will be compared against the list of winning numbers generated at random by computer. In the event that all prizes are not claimed, random drawings will be made from all entries received from all presentations to award all unclaimed prizes. All cash prizes are payable in U.S. funds. This is in addition to any free, surprise or mystery gifts that might be offered. The following prizes are awarded in this sweepstakes:

(1)	*Grand Prize	$1,000,000	Annuity
(1)	First Prize	$35,000	
(1)	Second Prize	$10,000	
(3)	Third Prize	$5,000	
(10)	Fourth Prize	$1,000	
(25)	Fifth Prize	$500	
(5000)	Sixth Prize	$5	

*The Grand Prize is payable through a $1,000,000 annuity. Winner may elect to receive $25,000 a year for 40 years, totaling up to $1,000,000 without interest, or $350,000 in one cash payment. Winners selected will receive the prizes offered in the Sweepstakes promotion they receive.

Entrants may cancel the Reader Service privileges at any time without cost or obligation to buy (see details in center insert card).

3. Versions of this Sweepstakes with different graphics may be offered in other mailings or at retail outlets by Torstar Corp. and its affiliates. This promotion is being conducted under the supervision of Marden-Kane, Inc., an independent judging organization. By entering this Sweepstakes, each entrant accepts and agrees to be bound by these rules and the decisions of the judges, which shall be final and binding. Odds of winning are dependent upon the total number of entries received. Taxes, if any, are the sole responsibility of the winners. Prizes are nontransferable. All entries must be received by March 31, 1990. The drawing will take place on April 30, 1990, at the offices of Marden-Kane, Inc., Lake Success, N.Y.

4. This offer is open to residents of the U.S., Great Britain and Canada, 18 years or older, except employees of Torstar Corp., its affiliates, and subsidiaries, Marden-Kane, Inc. and all other agencies and persons connected with conducting this Sweepstakes. All federal, state and local laws apply. Void wherever prohibited or restricted by law.

5. Winners will be notified by mail and may be required to execute an affidavit of eligibility and release that must be returned within 14 days after notification. Canadian winners will be required to answer a skill-testing question. Winners consent to the use of their name, photograph and/or likeness for advertising and publicity in conjunction with this and similar promotions without additional compensation. One prize per family or household.

6. For a list of our most current major prizewinners, send a stamped, self-addressed envelope to: WINNERS LIST, c/o MARDEN-KANE, INC., P.O. BOX 701, SAYREVILLE, N.J. 08871

If Sweepstakes entry form is missing, please print your name and address on a 3" ×5" piece of plain paper and send to:

In the U.S.

Sweepstakes Entry
901 Fuhrmann Blvd.
P.O. Box 1867
Buffalo, NY 14269-1867

In Canada

Sweepstakes Entry
P.O. Box 609
Fort Erie, Ontario
L2A 5X3

LTY-S69R

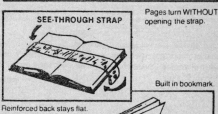
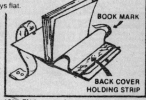

COMING NEXT MONTH

#535 NO SURRENDER—Lindsay McKenna
Navy pilot Alyssa Trayhern's assignment with arrogant jet jockey
Clay Cantrell threatens her pride, her career—and her heart—with a
crash landing. Book Two of Lindsay McKenna's gripping LOVE
AND GLORY series.

#536 A TENDER SILENCE—Karen Keast
Former POW Kell Chaisson knew all about survival. He'd brave
Bangkok's dangers to help Anne Elise Butler trace her MIA
husband's fate, but would he survive loving another man's wife?

#537 THORNE'S WIFE—Joan Hohl
Jonas Thorne was accomplished, powerful, devastatingly attractive.
Valerie Thorne loved her husband, but what would it take to convince
domineering Jonas that she was a person, not simply his wife?

#538 LIGHT FOR ANOTHER NIGHT—Anne Lacey
Wildlife biologist Brittany Hagen loved the wolves on primeval Isle
Svenson . . . until she encountered the two-legged variety—in the
person of ferociously attractive, predatory Paul Johnson.

#539 EMILY'S HOUSE—Nikki Benjamin
Vowing to secretly support widowed Emily Anderson and her child,
Major Joseph Cortez rented rooms in her house. But, hiding a guilty
secret, could he ever gain entrance to Emily's heart?

#540 LOVE THIS STRANGER—Linda Shaw
Pregnant nutritionist Mary Smith unwittingly assumed another
woman's identity when she accepted a job with the Olympic ski team.
Worse, she also "inherited" devastating Dr. Jed Kilpatrick—the
other woman's lover!

AVAILABLE THIS MONTH:

#529 A QUESTION OF HONOR
Lindsay McKenna

#530 ALL MY TOMORROWS
Debbie Macomber

#531 KING OF HEARTS
Tracy Sinclair

#532 FACE VALUE
Celeste Hamilton

#533 HEATHER ON THE HILL
Barbara Faith

#534 REPEAT PERFORMANCE
Lynda Trent